倍斯特出版事業有限公司
BEST BOOKS
Best Publishing Ltd.

Amazing yet practical

跟著小吃
用英語

林昭菁 ◎著

U0077337

晒台灣

品嚐「頂級美食」
用英語聊小吃，重拾你遺忘許久的味蕾

▽【景點報報】 詳盡介紹**最具代表性**的台灣好風光，帶你遠離都市塵囂、沉
浸在悠閒的自然氣息裡！

▽【小吃人氣報報】 了解台灣古早味的起源，一同尋訪最真實的**老味道**！

▽【外國人都是這樣問】 以最道地的英語聊喜愛小吃的**口味**、體會故鄉人
情味和了解小吃製作的趣味！

▽【美食報馬仔】 美食好去處報給你知，品嚐精湛手藝來趟**知性文藝之旅**！

MP3

Author and Editor
作者序和編者序

　　對我和我先生來說，台灣是很特別的地方，因為那是我們領養的孩子所出生的地方。我們是歐洲裔美國人，我們收養了來自台灣的三個兄妹。透過這本書的合著，我有機會研究以及書寫關於台灣食物。讀者可以透過這本書學習有關台灣的獨特食物以及認識幾個世紀以來外國強權在台灣對台灣食物的影響。讀者也可趁機一窺究竟台灣人民的生活型態，就像當年我們到台灣去接孩子一樣有機會學習有關台灣的事。我和先生當年在中秋節的前幾天逛了高雄夜市。當時有兩個台灣女生帶我們去逛夜市。有很多的原因值得我們珍惜這個記憶裡夜市的特別氣味，壅擠的人潮，發亮的中文英文廣告看板，以及好多好好吃的東西。

　　去夜市的幾天前我們剛從美國飛到台灣，我們終於見到透過領養加入我們家庭的孩子們。就在一年多前，我們完成領養文件，寄了禮物給孩子，也與孩子們有幾次網路面對面的接觸。我們還學了中文，並把家裡準備好要迎接一家五口的生活。感覺一下子我們就到了孩子們住的國度。在我們離開高雄之前，孩子們的英語輔導老師和社工堅持要帶我們去夜市逛逛。他們與我們在飯店見面後帶我們坐著充滿藝術視覺的捷運到夜市 。當時這兩名女生幫我們照第一個全家福，這也成為我們全家在一起的珍貴紀念照。

　　我可以感受為什麼他們堅持要帶我們去逛夜市，因為他們很關照我們的孩子，所以要讓孩子吃好吃的東西。他們甚至買了剉冰讓我們帶回飯店吃。我當時可以看得出來我們的新朋友是想讓外國父母體驗夜市在台灣日常生活的重要地位。時光飛逝，五年過去了，一家五口的生活讓我們更加珍惜這三個來自台灣的孩子。寫這本書讓我有機會深度的認識台灣，原來我記憶裡的夜市就是真正一般台灣人所吃的東西，夜市也幾乎是每個台灣人的成長記憶。我們知道，有機會再拜訪這個美麗的島嶼，我們一定會去夜市逛逛。

Taiwan is special to me and my husband because that is where our children were born. We are European-Americans who adopted three Taiwanese siblings. By co-writing this book, I had the opportunity to research and write about Taiwanese foods. This book provides information about unique Taiwanese foods. Readers can also learn about the influence of foreign powers throughout the centuries on Taiwanese foods, and get a glimpse of the lifestyle of the Taiwanese people as we did on our very important trip to Taiwan. During the week of the Autumn Moon Festival, my husband and I explored one of the night markets in Kaohsiung, guided by two local young women. Unusual smells, the crush of people, lighted signs in traditional Mandarin characters and in English – and so much delicious food. This was an experience to remember for many reasons.

We had arrived in Taipei just a couple of days before from the US, scheduled at last to meet the children who were joining our family by adoption. For over a year prior, we had completed paperwork, sent gifts and enjoyed the occasional teleconference with the kids. We had also studied Mandarin and prepared our home to shelter a family of five.Suddenly, we were together on their turf. The children's English language tutor and their social worker had insisted on escorting us to the night market before we left Kaohsiung. They met us at our hotel and led us to the market, via the city's art-filled subway. That's where these ladies snapped our first family portrait – a treasured souvenir of our very first days together.

It was clear to me why our guides wanted to take us to the market so urgently: These generous young women loved our children and lavished them with unique local snacks – even sending us back to the hotel with melting, bagged-up dishes of shaved ice for later. I could tell our kind new friends also wanted us foreign parents to understand the market's important position in daily life in Taiwan. Time flies and five years have passed by. We love our Taiwanese children more than anything. By co-writing this book, I had the chance to read more information about Taiwan. My memory of a night market in Taiwan is the true refection of daily food that people eat. Almost everyone who grows up in Taiwan has their own night market experience. No doubt the market will be a frequent stop for us every time we return to the Beautiful Island.

Angela 敬上

Contents 目次

Part 1

北台灣的文化風情

Part 2

中台灣的魅力風情

Part 3

南台灣的熱力風情

Part 4

東台灣農村風情

Part 1

北台灣的文化風情

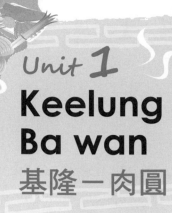

Unit 1
Keelung
Ba wan
基隆－肉圓

 Attractions 景點報報

基隆有十餘處砲台遺跡是早期守護台灣北部的港口，大武崙砲台、白米甕砲台、獅球嶺砲台、二沙灣砲台、槓子寮砲台現都被列為國家古蹟。但其實有些砲台都已經荒廢了。基隆曾經有多次的外敵入侵，在此留下痕跡的有日本人、西班牙人、荷蘭人、英國人還有法國人。西元 1884 年法軍曾佔領基隆長達八個月，和民族英雄墓相鄰的法國公墓，就是「中法戰爭」的歷史見證。基隆的獅球嶺隧道是台灣第一條鐵路隧道。

Popular snacks / street food 人氣小吃報報

Ba-wan can be called Taiwanese meatball, or meatball dumpling, depending on who you ask. It is a clear, stretchy rice flour-based dough wrapped around pork, bamboo shoots, and mushrooms, the whole measuring 6-8 centimeters in diameter. Ba-wan can be fried or steamed, or sometimes steamed, then fried to create a skin on the outside. The sauce is usually a sweet and spicy addition to the flavorful and interesting dumpling. This dish is easily available at night markets around Taiwan. Its earliest beginnings are thought to be in Changhua County. Its ingredients consist mainly of those that grow naturally in Taiwan: rice, sweet potatoes, bamboo shoots, pork (or wild boar), and dried mushrooms. These simple ingredients may have been those that were most easily accessible during austere times around the turn of the 20th century. The dish appeared during that time, near the end of the Qing Dynasty in Taiwan and just before the Japanese empire spread to the island in 1912. Today, the most famous place to try ba-wan is A Ling Ba-wan in Keelung. It tastes very fresh and not greasy. A Ling's ba-wan also has the ideal "ba-wan skin." It is chewy but easy to chew, bringing deepness to the taste.

 中譯

就看你發問的是誰，肉圓在英文裡有不同的說法，如台灣肉丸或肉丸餃子。是以一種用在來米粉做成的麵團，裡面包裹著豬肉、竹筍和香菇。一粒肉圓大小約有 4－6 公分的直徑。肉圓可以用炸的或蒸的，或有時蒸熟後再炸，讓外皮酥脆。肉圓的醬通常是甜辣醬可以讓美味的肉圓更夠味。這道小吃在台灣各地夜市都很容易買的到。肉圓最早的起源被認為是在彰化縣。肉圓的成分主要包括在台灣的自然食材：米、地瓜、竹筍、豬肉（或野豬肉）和香菇。這些簡單的材料都是 20 世紀初，在台灣物資嚴峻的時代可容易取得的材料。這道小吃的出現剛好在台灣的清末與日本帝國 1912 年開始佔領全台前。在基隆最有名的肉圓是「阿玲肉圓」。「阿玲肉圓」內餡很清爽不油膩。阿玲肉圓的皮也具有理想中的肉圓皮，有嚼勁又很容易咬，讓口感豐富了許多。

Q & A 外國人都是這樣問 ◉)) *MP3 01*

Q1 **I'm not so sure about that shiny, translucent part of the meatball. Is it fat?**
我不確定要不要吃那種看起來亮亮的、半透明圓圓的肉圓？油脂很高嗎？

A This is a starchy dough made of sweet potato flour and cornstarch or rice flour and tapioca flour. It is only fatty because it is deep fried.

My favorite street vendor for ba-wan takes it out of the pan of fry oil, cuts it open and uses a wooden fork to squeeze out the extra grease before it is served. It tastes good but I am sure it is not good if you want to be on a diet.

這種肉圓的皮是混合地瓜粉、太白粉、或在來米粉、樹薯粉做成的。吃起來很肥是因為油炸過。

我最喜歡的肉圓攤，老闆在油鍋裡撈了肉圓後，再送餐前會用剪刀將肉圓剪開，接著用木叉子將肉圓多餘的油壓出來。很好吃，但我想，對減肥來說沒有好處。

12

B Its texture is a little bit like fat, but it's not fat at all. It is closer to a bread or noodle in function. The ingredients and preparation make for a chewy, jelly-like eating experience.

這個口感吃起來好像有點油油的，但其實一點也不油。有點接近麵包或麵條。混合的粉料和做法讓肉圓吃起來很有嚼勁，很像在吃果凍。

C No, it's not fat. It's just a steamed dough. I think it's the cornstarch in the recipe that makes it look a little translucent like fat.

不會。不會很油。這只是一種蒸過的麵團。我覺得是因為裡面加了太白粉，所以看起來有點半透明，有點油油的。

Q2 What kind of sauce is this? Does it always have cilantro on top?

沾醬是什麼？一般都會撒上香菜嗎？

A This reddish sauce is tomato-based sweet and sour sauce that includes soy sauce, vinegar, and sugar. Yes. I love cilantro. It has a subtle taste but the combination is perfectly satisfying.

這紅紅的沾醬是以番茄為主的酸甜，由醬油、醋和糖一起熬煮。是的，我很喜歡香菜，香菜有特殊的味道，但這樣的組合很完美。

B Each vendor makes their own special sauce. The sauce I like is a clearer sauce that is mainly citrus juice, soy, vinegar, and sugar.

每個商家都有自己特別的醬汁。我喜歡的是一種顏色較透明的醬汁，主要由柑橘類果汁、醬油、醋和糖所調成。

C You can choose either the tomato-based sauce or the citrus-based sauce. Both are sweet and sour and include soy sauce, vinegar, and sugar.

你可以選擇番茄醬或柑橘醬。這兩種都酸酸甜甜的，因為材料裡都有醬油、醋和糖。

1 北台灣的文化風情

2 中台灣的魅力風情

3 南台灣的熱力風情

4 東台灣農村風情

Q3 Are there differences in ba-wan's preparation or ingredients, depending on where you purchase it?

肉圓的做法或材料是否因為購買地的不一有所不同嗎？

A Yes, but only minor differences are common, since the island of Taiwan is so small.

是的，但通常只有輕微的差異，因為台灣畢竟是個小島。

B Yes. Traditionally, in Changua city where they originated – Beidou – ba-wan are steamed and then "poached" in hot oil to give the dough a skin and a translucent sheen. But in other cities, the ba- wan may only be steamed or only fried.

是的。傳統上，在肉圓的起源地方——彰化市北斗，肉圓是在蒸熟後再放到熱油裡煮，這樣的肉圓看起來才會透亮光澤，但是，在其他城市，肉圓通常是用蒸的或炸的。

C Yes, and in Changua County, you can even get them served in a cold broth in the summer. People like to have a bowl of clear soup to eat with ba-wan, such as fish ball soup or squid soup. My favorite is chopped squid covered with fish paste added to clear broth and topped with minced celery. That's the best.

是的，夏天時，你甚至可以在彰化縣買到肉圓是放在冷湯裡一起吃的。一般人在吃肉圓時喜歡點湯配著吃。如魚丸湯或魷魚羹。我最喜歡的湯是魚漿包覆著魷魚，加入沒有勾芡的湯頭中，再加點芹菜就是最棒的。

Information 美食報馬仔

基隆廟口外的基隆孝三路 99 巷內三個攤子分別賣肉圓、魷魚羹、長腳麵食是在地人才知道的巷弄美食，這三個攤子是連在一起的，肉圓、魷魚 都只有賣單一品項，長腳麵食則賣有各式的麵食、湯，還有豬腳與小菜。孝三路的大腸圈也是巷弄內的古早味極品美食。豬心、豬肺、豬舌，這個 40 多年的小攤賣的是手工的香腸，大腸圈是用真正的大腸所灌的。大腸圈旁的四神湯和包子攤也是個好選擇。

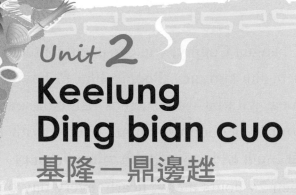

Unit 2
Keelung
Ding bian cuo
基隆－鼎邊趖

Attractions 景點報報

在台灣有港口的地方就有廟宇，位於基隆市仁三路旁的奠濟宮是基隆三大廟之一，奠濟宮就在基隆廟口裡。基隆港是早期台灣的重要港口，附近從流動攤販漸漸形成基隆廟口夜市，從愛二路至愛三路之間的仁三路，不到 400 公尺就有近 200 個攤位，各種具有代表性的台灣小吃都可以在這裡吃到。每到傍晚時分這裡就會燈火通明，照亮基隆一整夜，這裡感受到台灣美食的魅力與平民小吃的實在感。

Popular snacks / street food 人氣小吃報報

Ding bian cuo is a soup of slippery rice noodles and condiments. The noodles are made by coating a hot wok with thin noodle batter and then cutting up the results to make chewy, thin sheet-like noodles. Noodles float in a surprisingly delicious broth of shrimp paste, napa cabbage, celery, and fried shallots. Sometimes the broth also has dried mushrooms, bamboo shoots, dried tiger lily, dried shrimp, shredded pork, or oysters. Keelung's Miaokow Night Market – Miaokow meaning "in front of the temple" – is one of the oldest and most famous places to eat ding bian cuo. Wu Jia ding bian cuo is the family business inside the market that has been making the soup for over 100 years. This night market dates from the end of the Japanese occupation when the Dianji Temple was severely damaged by a torpedo, but was quickly repaired. The market is open 24 hours a day, nearly every day of the year. Such a famous market receives a lot of international tourists, so the market strives to be tourist friendly with signs in Traditional Mandarin, Japanese, and English. They have a website that has most information available in English including market history and lists of vendors: www.miaokow.org.

 中譯

　　鼎邊趖是由滑潤粉皮加調味料的湯麵。粉皮的做法是在熱鐵鍋的鍋邊塗上一層薄薄的米糊，蒸烤後切下來，做出有嚼勁的、薄片般的粉皮。鍋邊趖驚人地美味湯頭材料有加蝦醬、白菜、芹菜和炒過的紅蔥頭。有時湯汁也會加香菇、竹筍、金針、乾蝦仁，肉絲，或牡蠣。基隆廟口夜市裡有一攤最古早、最有名的　邊趖攤位－廟口指廟的前方。有 100 年歷史的「百年吳家鼎邊銼」就在廟口夜市裡。基隆廟口夜市在日據時代末期就形成了，當時奠濟宮遭到魚雷嚴重損壞，但很快就被修復。這個市場不僅僅是一個夜市。更是個全天全年幾乎每天 24 小時營運的夜市。這樣一個著名的市場受到了很多國際遊客的喜愛，為了讓觀光客更加容易辨別每個攤位都標有中、日、英三個名稱。他們有一個網站裡有列出攤販的英文資料和歷史：www.miaokow.org。

Q & A 外國人都是這樣問 🔊)) *MP3 02*

Q1 **How does the chef make these large thin noodles?**

那種薄薄大大的麵是怎麼做的呢？

A At the night market, you can watch the noodles being made. Do you want to see for yourself?

在夜市裡，你可以看他們怎麼做麵，你想要看看嗎？

B The chef uses a small bowl to spread a thin layer of batter on the surface of a hot wok. The noodle cooks quickly, then it can be cut or broken into these large sheets and dropped into the broth for cooking.

廚師會把一碗米糊沿著熱鍋邊薄薄的滾一圈，米糊會煮得很快，然後就可以拿出來剪成一片片放入湯裡。

C The chef pours rice paste onto the side of the wok, covers it with the lid which then bakes and steams it at once. He then scrapes the cooked noodles off of the walls of the wok and puts it in the soup to cook. It makes sense since ding bian cuo literally translates to "potside sticker soup."

廚師會把一碗米漿從鍋子的邊邊倒下，蓋上鍋蓋子，同時烘烤與炊蒸。麵好了後就慢慢的把麵從鍋子的邊邊刮下來放入湯裡。這是很有道理的，因為「鼎邊趖」字面上的意思就是「黏在鍋邊的湯」。

Q2 Why does soup on a hot day even sound like a good idea to the locals?
為什麼很熱的天氣當地人還會想喝熱湯呢？

A I don't know, but the people of many East Asian countries with warm climates eat soup daily, often for breakfast like congee or for a snack like ding bian cuo.

我不知道，但許多位在氣候溫暖的東亞國家每天都會喝湯，通常像早餐吃粥或像鼎邊趖這種小吃。

B In traditional Chinese medicine, taking hot liquids is considered beneficial to a person's health, and by contrast – especially if a person is fighting a cold – having cold drinks or food like ice cream is considered foolish and thought to have a negative effect on health.

就傳統中國醫學上來說，喝熱飲被認為對人的健康有益。相反的，特別是要對抗感冒時喝冷飲或吃冰淇淋被認為是非常不智的，且對健康有負面影響。

C At the night market, the day is cooling off and eating hot soup keeps us warm.

在夜市，一天的結束之際剛好是天氣降溫的時候，喝熱湯會讓我們感到暖和。

Q3 Do people make Ding bian cuo at home?
一般人會在家自己做鼎邊趖嗎？

A I don't think so. Actually, I have never tasted Ding bian cuo before. It just does not appeal to me.

我不知道。我不認為。事實上我沒有吃過鼎邊趖，那不是很吸引我。

B Wu Jia ding bian cuo can be ordered online and it is not bad. It does not have preservatives and you can eat it in the comfort of your own home.

百年吳家鼎邊銼可以網購，還不錯吃。這樣的網購鼎邊銼不含防腐劑，也可以在家舒服的吃。

C At least in Tainan where I grew up, there does not seem to be the tradition of using rice flour to make big noodles. However, the ingredients in the soup base are very common ingredients used all over Taiwan, especially dried mushroom, bamboo shoots, fried shallots, dried tiger lily, celery, napa, dried shrimp, shredded and dried squid and little dried fish.

至少在我生長的台南，鼎邊銼不是很熟悉的食物。台南這個地方好像沒有在用在來米粉做大麵條的。然而，湯底的材料用的是台灣非常普遍的食材，即香菇、筍絲、蒜頭酥、金針、芹菜、高麗菜、蝦米、魷魚絲和小魚乾。

 ## *Information* 美食報馬仔

人山人海的基隆廟口夜市有好幾百個攤位，第 41 攤就是著名的「陳記泡泡冰」，綿密的冰融入泥狀花生就是有名的泡泡冰。第 9 攤是的「營養三明治」是屬於古早味三明治。第 19 攤是日間光復肉羹，第 21 攤是魯排骨，第 31 攤是天一香肉羹順，第 36 攤是炭燒蚵仔煎，第 16 攤是有名老店刑記鼎邊趖，第 66 攤是油粿、芋頭粿。很多攤位也都有提供座位區。

Unit 3
Taipei
braised pork rice
台北－滷肉飯

Attractions 景點報報

　　台北市中正紀念堂捷運車站有七個出口。出口 5 可到中正紀念堂，出口 6 可到國家圖書館，出口 2 可到南門市場、南海路。位在羅斯福路一段的南門市場是南北貨聚集地，這裡的周邊美食樣樣齊全。在南門市場與中正紀念堂二號出口旁的金峰魯肉飯，是大台北地區有名的滷肉飯。南海路有台灣歷史博物館，南海路往泉州街位在建國中學圍牆旁的泉州街「林家乾麵」與「建中黑糖剉冰」都是當地美食。

Popular snacks / street food 人氣小吃報報

Braised pork rice, or lu rou fan is a rather simple, yet satisfying dish. It consists of finely minced pork belly, braised in rich soy sauce, onions, and spices. Hard-boiled eggs may also simmer in the sauce, adding another layer of richness to this dish. The pork, the sauce, and the eggs are all served over steamed white rice. The best place to try lu rou fan in Taipei is called Jin Feng Lu Rou Fan. The Michelin Green Guide Taiwan of 2011 mistakenly credited China's Shandong province as the original home of lu rou fan. The mistake is related to the character used for "lu" – whether it should be the character for braised or its homonym meaning the ruling state of Shandong 2,000 years ago. Michelin translated lu rou fan as Lu (Shandong-Style) Meat Rice. The correct translation should be Braised pork rice. In 2011, Taipei City officials and restaurateurs were so upset about mainland China getting credit for the dish that they launched a promotional campaign, giving away 1,000 bowls of lu rou fan. Another mistake the Guide made is the description of the recipe "the pork fried with minced onion". Taiwan lu rou fan is never fried with minced onion. Cooks only use shallots to make it.

 中譯

　　滷肉飯是一道相當簡單卻讓人有滿足感的小吃。由切碎的五花肉與醬油、紅蔥末和調味料炒過後一起熬煮。煮好去殼的蛋也可放入一起滷可以添加風味。把熬煮好的肉燥在白飯淋上一瓢，就是滷肉飯。在臺北吃肉飯最棒的地方是金峰滷肉飯。2011 年出版的米其林台灣綠色指南錯誤記載滷肉飯起源於山東。這個錯誤涉及到「魯」和「滷」這兩個字，「滷」是指熬煮，「魯」則是 2000 年前山東的簡稱。在 2011 年，台北市官員和滷肉飯餐館老闆對於滷肉飯源自中國一事感到很氣憤，他們之後推出了促銷活動，就是贈送 1000 碗滷肉飯給市民，以此告知天下滷肉飯是台灣的原產。米其林指南更錯把食譜寫成加洋蔥炒製，正統台灣滷肉飯不曾使用洋蔥，只使用紅蔥頭。

Q1 **What types of spice are used in the braised pork and rice?**
滷肉飯通常使用的調味料是什麼？

A The spices can vary a little depending on the region.

滷肉飯的味道會因所在地和廚師的不同而有些差異。

B My grandmother made the best braised pork sauce for the braised pork and rice. Fried minced shallots and garlic are the key. When frying, the heat has to be low, so it does not burn. Another key ingredient is rock sugar. She cooked the rock sugar with water until it turns a brown color then she added the mixture to the braised pork sauce. Cook all together over low heat and eventually it will turn the nice amber color .

我阿嬤做的肉燥最好吃了。爆香紅蔥末跟蒜末是關鍵，火一定要小，不要燒焦了。才能做出好的肉燥。另外一個重要的材料是冰糖，她都用水煮至呈咖啡色後再混合肉燥，以小火一起熬煮，最後就會鹵出來的汁是呈琥珀色。

C My mom's secret recipe for braised pork sauce is soy sauce, salt, Chinese Five-Spice powder and peanut butter. Peanut butter gives the beautiful amber color.

我媽媽做肉燥的秘方是醬油、鹽、五香粉和花生醬。花生醬加醬油可以讓肉燥看起來是漂亮的琥珀色。

1 北台灣的文化風情

2 中台灣的魅力風情

3 南台灣的熱力風情

4 東台灣農村風情

Is this a dish that local Taiwanese people eat all the time? It's so high in fat.

這是台灣人常吃的小吃嗎？這看起來是油脂很高的菜。

A It's not special for holidays. It is a common food that many people eat on regular basis because it is cheap, it is satisfying and many places sell it.

這是平民小吃，因為便宜，很多人是固定常吃，因為吃起來很有飽足感，而且很多地方都有賣。

B Yes. I would say that braised pork rice for most Taiwanese people is like hamburger or sandwiches for most Americans.

是的。我覺得對大多數台灣人來說滷肉飯就好像是大多數美國人常吃的漢堡或三明治。

C The major difference in Taiwanese eating habits is that they eat more clear broths, eat more slowly to be satisfied, and eat less sugar and dessert. Some of these habits are changing as western influences increase.

在台灣，主要的飲食習慣區別在，他們喜歡喝比較清的肉湯，慢慢地吃到有滿足感，比較少吃糖類和甜食。但是現在因為西方的影響，有些飲食習慣都變了。

1 北台灣的文化風情

2 中台灣的魅力風情

3 南台灣的熱力風情

4 東台灣農村風情

Q3 Does your family make braised pork rice?
你的家人常常做滷肉飯嗎？

A Yes, this would be a common evening meal for our family when I was growing up, and I loved how the aroma of the simmering stew filled the house while I did my homework. For me, braised pork rice brings back memories of my mom.

是的，小時候我們家晚餐常常吃這個。我做功課時，很喜歡聞到整個房子瀰漫那股香氣。對我來説，滷肉飯就是媽媽的味道。

B I usually make it myself. After frying the minced pork, add pepper and all spice and sauté, then add soy sauce, shallot, rice wine and rock sugar. Add broth and soy sauce paste, turn down to low heat, cover and cook for 40 minutes.

我都是自己做肉燥。五花肉丁炒過後，加入胡椒粉和五香粉炒香，再加入醬油、紅蔥頭，米酒、冰糖炒入味，加入高湯和醬油膏，轉小火並蓋上鍋蓋煮 40 分鐘即可。

C My mom makes something similar-a braised sauce without meat. She used diced firm soybean tofu instead of meat. With meat or not, soy sauce and shallots are the key for such a braised sauce.

我媽媽會做類似的素肉燥。她會放豆干和大豆煮成素肉燥。有沒有肉都沒關係,醬油和紅蔥頭才是重點。

 ## *Information* 美食報馬仔

　　中正紀念堂捷運站美食人氣最夯的是高三孝碳烤吐司、豆味行還有鹹酥雞。高三孝位於南門市場正後方。高三孝的老闆「堅持帶給大家 80 年代的味道,樸實而單純」。豆味行剉冰、豆花與芋圓綠豆湯,還有片狀與條狀甜不辣、油豆腐,白蘿蔔,貢丸,魚丸等等。在豆味行附近還有一攤獨特的「閒酥雞」。老闆以前愛吃的鹹酥雞收攤了,就自己開起了「閒酥雞」。

Unit 4
Taipei
Iron egg
台北－鐵蛋

Attractions 景點報報

　　在淡水逛老街，走小巷、上階梯、下階梯和走岸邊可以感受小鎮的特色。中正路、真理街、重建街、三民街、清水街一帶有很多洋式的舊建築。淡水禮拜堂、理學堂大書院、淡江中學、馬偕博士發跡地、牧師樓與姑娘樓、真理大學、小白宮、紅毛城都靜靜地在敘說這個小鎮的歷史。淡水河岸景觀步道全長 1.5 公里是散步賞景的好地方。淡水老街有許多傳統美食，像是魚丸、魚酥、阿給、酸梅湯、石花凍、鐵蛋。

Popular snacks / street food 人氣小吃報報

Iron egg, fried fish cracker, and A-Gei (stuffed tofu) are local delicacies native to the northern fishing village of Danshui. The origins behind these foods tell stories of fish villagers' frugal way of life regarding not wasting any food. Iron egg is a way to preserve the eggs by re-cooking and re-serving leftover eggs. Fried fish cracker is also a way to preserve abundant fish caught in the river of Danshui at a time when there was no refrigeration system. The story behind A-Gei is a cook's reinvention from leftover scrap food. Iron eggs are made by simmering hard-boiled eggs in soy sauce and spices, then drying and repeating the process for several days. Because of the long cooking time, iron eggs are black or brownish-black and their texture is rubbery and tough. The locals love the chewy experience of enjoying an iron egg. Quail eggs are the traditional type of egg used to make iron eggs, so the resulting snack is much smaller than a conventional chicken egg. Danshui was not always the laid-back tourist-friendly town on the northern edge of Taipei, but once a focal point of Spanish settlement in the 1600s and then a key to Japan's colony on Taiwan during the first half of the 1900s.

 中譯

　　鐵蛋、魚酥、阿給這些美味都是原產於淡水北部的漁村。這些美食故事的背後都在訴說著早期漁村生活不想浪費任何食物的哲學。鐵蛋是一種以再煮過，或儲備剩蛋的方式來保存蛋，魚酥也是在彼時沒有冰箱的年代，為了保存從淡水河中所捕獲的漁獲而衍生的。阿給的由來是為了不想浪費賣剩下的食材所研發的獨特小吃。鐵蛋的作法是用醬油及五香配方的滷料煮過後，再風乾，此道程序要重覆幾天才算完成。因為長時間的滷煮，鐵蛋呈黑或黑褐色，口感有彈性且硬。當地人喜歡鐵蛋的嚼勁。傳統的鐵蛋是用鵪鶉蛋，這樣做出來的鐵蛋會比一般的雞蛋小很多。早期的淡水並非像現在給人的印象是台北北部的悠閒觀光小鎮，17 世紀時西班牙曾把這裡當殖民地，在 20 世紀上半葉時，日本人把這裡當成殖民台灣的一個關鍵的地方。

Q1 If I bite into this iron egg, am I going to find that it is a fertilized egg with a bird embryo inside?

如果我咬下這顆鐵蛋，會不會咬到裡面鳥的胚胎？

A You might be surprised by the rubbery quality of the egg, but I promise you there is no baby chick inside.

鐵蛋的咬勁對你來說可能很驚奇，但是絕不會有小雞在裡面。

B I don't know – maybe this possibility adds a sense of adventure to the experience!

我不知道。或許這樣添加了一種冒險的經驗！

C No, there is not a baby bird inside the egg. Perhaps you are thinking of a different dish from other countries in southeast Asia – called "balut." I have never tried balut, but I believe it is a duck fetus inside a shell.

不會啦，鐵蛋裡沒有胚胎。也許你想的是一種來自其他東南亞國家的菜——叫「巴魯特」，我是從來沒有吃過巴魯特，但我知道外殼內是有小鴨胚胎。

1 北台灣的文化風情

2 中台灣的魅力風情

3 南台灣的熱力風情

4 東台灣農村風情

Q2 What kind of eggs are iron eggs?
鐵蛋是什麼樣的蛋做的呢?

A There are several kinds of eggs that are deemed as delicacies, such as century eggs and iron eggs. Some prefer to have this dish with other dishes, such as tofu. Walking down Dan Shui street, you can see lots of shops selling iron eggs and several side dishes for you to choose from. These small ones are quail eggs, but the dish can also be made from chicken or pigeon eggs.

有幾種蛋被視為是佳餚,像是皮蛋和鐵蛋。有些人傾向吃鐵蛋搭配其他菜餚,像是豆腐。沿著淡水街頭走著,你能看到許多店家販售著鐵蛋和幾種副產品,可供你選擇。這些小的是鵪鶉蛋,但也可以拿雞或鴿子蛋來做鐵蛋。

B These are quail eggs. Have you ever eaten a quail egg?

這是鵪鶉蛋。你有沒有吃過鵪鶉蛋?

C Quail eggs taste very much like chicken eggs. Cholesterol and phospholipid content in quail eggs are higher than chicken eggs. My grandpa used to raise quails for eggs. The temperature has to be suitable for quails to lay eggs at a steady rate.

鵪鶉蛋的味道和一般雞蛋的味道非常像。鵪鶉蛋的膽固醇與磷脂含量含量都高於雞蛋。我阿公以前有養鵪鶉，室內溫度要適宜鵪鶉才能以穩定的速率產蛋。

Q3 I see vacuum packages of different colors where the shops sell iron eggs. Are these different flavors?

我在商店裡有看到真空包裝不同顏色的鐵雞蛋。這些味道不一樣嗎？

A Yes, common flavors offered are garlic, black pepper, and spicy. I love iron eggs. I heard that it takes a week to make iron eggs. There are no artificial additives. The taste is very unique.

是的，大眾口味是大蒜、黑胡椒及調味料。我聽說要花 1 個星期才能製作出香 Q 的鐵蛋。它不添加防腐劑，口味又相當獨特。

B Yes, I really prefer the garlic flavor, though many enjoy the salty and sweet combination of the black pepper flavored eggs.

是的，我真的很喜歡大蒜口味，雖然許多人可能喜歡鐵蛋裡黑胡椒的鹹中帶甜的組合。

C Yes, and all the flavors are good, but if you don't like spicy food, avoid buying the bright red and orange packages!

是的，所有的味道都不錯，但如果你不喜歡吃辣的食物，就不要買鮮紅色和橙色的包裝！

 ## Information 美食報馬仔

淡水商家最先把鐵蛋登記註冊商標稱為「阿婆鐵蛋」，但真正發明阿婆鐵蛋商家的註冊商標是「海邊鐵蛋」。老街的「阿香鳥蛋」鳥蛋加入 50 條小魚烤成一串，沾料吃。許義魚酥是狗母魚、黃魚、地瓜粉和醬料所做的特殊魚酥。阿給是用四方形油豆腐，中間填塞粉絲，用魚漿封口蒸熟，食用時淋上甜辣醬最夠味。正港阿給老店在真理街 6-1 號，即在淡水國中正門附近。淡水魚丸是用鯊魚肉與豬絞肉團所做。

Unit 5
Taoyuan
Chinese meat pie
桃園－餡餅

 ***Attractions* 景點報報**

　　桃園市龍潭區有分佈密集的茶園，龍泉茶就是桃園的茶葉，大溪豆干是來自桃園市大溪區。桃園的大自然景點很豐富，有拉拉山(達觀山)自然保護區、桃源仙谷、慈湖兩蔣文化行館、角板山公園、竹圍漁港、宇內溪瀑布群、經國梅園、虎頭山環保公園、石門水庫風景區。桃園市觀光夜市位於中正一街、正康二街及北埔路上。位於桃園大溪鎮的大溪老街是充滿歷史懷舊風情的老街。

 ***Popular snacks / street food* 人氣小吃報報**

Chinese meat pie is a simple, tasty snack of dough, filled with pork or beef and vegetables: onions or green onion, etc. Also in the meat mixture are traditional spices and flavors: soy sauce, ginger, garlic, eggs, sesame oil, pepper, salt, and sometimes monosodium glutamate. After the cook makes the simple wheat dough, he adds raw beef mixture, wraps dough around beef and pan fries 3-4 minutes per side. The result is a lovely, compact, round packet that is crispy on the top and bottom, soft on the sides, and really juicy on the inside. Common Chinese meat pies you can buy in Taiwan are a round shape, about 10 cm in diameter. Many foods from China come with a myth about how the food originated. In the case of Chinese Meat Pie, there are stories about an emperor who disguised himself in order to sample the rustic, local fare. He thought the xiang-he pies were so delicious, and so much better than what he was served at the palace. He even commemorated the flavor with a hastily scribed poem.

 中譯

　　餡餅是一種很簡單好吃的小吃，基本上是麵團裡包入豬肉餡或牛肉餡，加入蔬菜洋蔥或蔥等。另外在肉裡也會加入傳統的調料和香料：醬油、薑、蒜頭、雞蛋、香油、鹽，有時也會加味精。麵團做好後就可包入肉餡，然後兩邊各煎 3-4 分鐘即可。這樣就做出了小巧、紮實，上下表皮都酥脆，內餡柔軟多汁的圓餡餅。台灣攤販所賣的餡餅通常是一個 10 公分大小的圓形。很多中國食品的起源都有點神話般。就餡餅來說，有一個皇帝把自己喬裝就為了要品嚐當地的美食。他覺得餡餅很好吃，而且比任何他在皇殿裡的端上來的食物好吃多了。他甚至還匆匆的自己寫下一首詩來回味這個味道。

Q1 **How does the cook make such a nice crust?**
這麼好吃的麵皮是怎麼做的呢？

Ⓐ That is the cook's secret. If he tells you how to make your own, why would you come to his shop to buy some?

那是廚師的秘密。如果他告訴你怎麼自己做，你為什麼還要去他的店裡買？

Ⓑ It's good, isn't it? I believe one reason the pastry is soft and crispy is the use of high gluten or bread flour in the dough, and both hot and cold water.

很好吃對不對？我覺得麵皮軟又脆的其中一個秘密是用了高筋麵粉，並同時加了滾水和冷水。

Ⓒ An experienced cook knows just the right amount of liquid to add to the flour and is patient to wait for the dough to rest before attempting to roll it out.

There is a "golden ratio" for water and flour. My recipe uses three cups of flour, a half cup of boiling water and a half cup of cold water. Add the boiling water to the flour, quickly stir it with chopsticks. Add the cold water and knead the dough until smooth.

有經驗的人都知道麵團最重要的是麵粉與水的比例，還有再擀麵團前一定要耐心地等候麵團鬆弛。

水和麵粉是有黃金比例的，我用的食譜是三杯麵粉、半杯熱水、半杯冷水。把熱水倒入麵粉後，快速的用筷子和水攪拌麵團，再倒入冷水後把麵團揉均勻即可。

Do you prefer the beef or pork version?
你比較喜歡牛肉餡或豬肉餡呢?

A Meat pies are definitely on people's must-have food list. Some people think vegetarian meat pies provide a simple and earthy flavor, while others prefer to actually have real meat in it. Some gourmet editors value highly the properly seasoned meat and a perfect crust. I couldn't possibly choose one over the other. I like both and the vegetarian version as well.

肉派確實在人們食物清單上。有些人認為素食餡餅提供了簡單且平凡的感覺,而其他人偏好真的有實實在在的肉在餅裡頭。有些美食家編輯們則極重視適度調味的肉品和完美的外層。我沒辦法選擇哪一個比較好。我都喜歡,素食也不錯。

B The pork one reminds me of my family and the traditional, simple food my mother made at home. Pork is an ingredient that you find a lot in Taiwanese dishes.

豬肉餡讓我想起了我的家人,和我媽媽在家裡常做的傳統、簡單的食物。大部分台灣菜的料理都是用豬肉。

C For me, it depends on what other flavors are included. I really love the ones with lots of scallions.

I also like the combined flavor of ginger and garlic. Some people don't add garlic.

對我來說，我覺得要看餡裡面加的其他材料是什麼。我很喜歡有加很多蔥花的。

我也很喜歡有加入薑與蒜頭的。有些餡餅沒有加蒜頭。

Q3 How is the stuffing inside meat pies different from potstickers?

餡餅與煎餃的內餡有什麼不一樣？

A It is similar. Usually chopped napa or cabbage are added to potstickers. Meat pies mostly use just onion or green onion.

很類似。煎餃的內餡會用切碎的大白菜或高麗菜。餡餅通常只有加洋蔥或蔥。

B I think they are all similar but somehow different. Actually the real difference is the shape. Meat pie is round and flat. Potstickers are like dumplings standing up.

我覺得這兩種很類似卻又不同。我覺得真正不同的是形狀。餡餅是圓圓扁扁的。煎餃像水餃是站立的。

C My mom always says they are similar. Meat pie is bigger and potstickers are smaller. If she is cooking for many people, she makes meat pies so just a few for each person is plenty of food. If she is making just for her and my dad, she makes potstickers.

我媽媽總是説他們很類似。餡餅比較大，煎餃比較小。如果她要做給很多人吃，她會做餡餅，所以每個只吃幾個就會很飽。如果她只是做給她和我爸爸吃，她就會做煎餃。

 ## Information 美食報馬仔

在桃園市中山東路上必吃的是老家餡餅與陸軍小館。老家餡餅賣的是餡餅、涼麵和薏仁。原本只是流動餐車的老家餡餅現在有店面了。因為真材實料如同招牌的廣告語一樣「皮薄餡多，湯鮮味美」而成為當地美食。陸軍小館讓人感受眷村氣息，也激起很多人當時反攻大陸氛圍的印象。此店家賣的都是麵類與小菜。光是菜名「陸軍乾拌麵」就很吸引人會讓人想試試。

Unit 6
Taoyuan
Shaved ice mountain
桃園－刨冰山

 Attractions 景點報報

桃園的客家文化館位於桃園龍潭區，這是一個完整保存客家風俗民情，讓大眾了解客家音樂與文學的文化館。三坑老街位於桃園龍潭三坑子，早期被稱為龍潭第一街。三坑老街中有客家傳統物品與美食，像是南瓜飯、客家菜包、紅龜粿、草仔粿、客家肉粽和蘿蔔糕。永福宮位於老街底，附近的青錢第古厝建於 1894 年，鄰村是大平聚落，大平聚落窄又彎曲的巷道是客家庄建築特色。

Popular snacks / street food 人氣小吃報報

Bao Bing is "a dessert made of shaved or finely crushed ice with flavoring." It is called Tsu Bing in Taiwanese. It makes sense to call it "Shaved Ice" in English. In general, shaved ice mountain consists of a big pile of tiny ice pieces, topped with sweet fruit like mango and sweetened condensed milk. The ice itself is incredibly fine and more similar to snow than crushed ice. A more traditional version is smaller and includes tapioca balls. It's quite easy to find shaved ice mountain with every variety of fruit imaginable, sweetened red beans, taro root, sweet potato and tapioca pearls. Another common and unique topping for shaved ice mountain is aiyu jelly. Aiyu jelly is made from a type of fig found in Taiwan, though the jelly has little flavor of its own. It just adds a wiggly, squishy texture to the popular dessert. Another very unique and traditional shaved ice is banana ice. There were no fancy toppings in the olden days when resources were very limited. Banana ice is just water mixed with sugar and banana flavoring. Freeze the mixture to form a big square ice then shave it finely. That is the old time favorite banana ice.

 中譯

　　刨冰就是一種「削薄的冰上面加調味的甜點」，台語又稱為剉冰。用英文「Shaved Ice」來翻譯這個美食是很有道理的。一般的刨冰就是將冰切細後在冰的上面加上水果如芒果和煉乳。刨冰的冰是刨得很綿細，比冰塊還像雪片。有些更傳統的冰更是在綿細冰上面加上粉圓。刨冰的配料有各種水果、紅豆、芋頭、甜番薯、粉圓和珍珠都可以加。另一種常見和獨特的配料是愛玉凍。愛玉果凍是由一種在台灣生長的一種無花果所製成的，這種果凍有很特殊的味道。加了愛玉的冰吃起來有軟軟的口感很受歡迎。香蕉冰是另一種很傳統也很特別的味道。以前物資缺少的年代是加上這麼多料的冰，通常是用最便宜的用料作出最好吃的風味，於是在清冰裡加了食用性香蕉水拌入白砂糖，結凍後，即可刨成可口的香蕉冰。

Q1 **Does the ice itself have milk in it?**
刨冰本身有加牛奶嗎？

A No, not the traditional shaved ice mountain – it's just ice with whatever toppings plus sweetened condensed milk or brown syrup.

沒有，傳統的刨冰只是冰上面加甜煉乳或糖水。

B It's not like ice cream at all-just frozen water, shaved and topped with whatever fruit you like and then sweetened condensed milk.

這個跟冰淇淋一點都不像，刨冰只是冰凍的水，刨下來，然後淋上任何你喜歡的配料，再加上煉乳。

C In movies, there were various versions of shaved ice that were used to convey a nostalgic feeling, either in the scene where the chemistry between actor and heroine sparks, or a loving father bringing home shaved ice for kids after being away from home for so long. More modern versions have been created that do have milk frozen in the ice, but the traditional version is just ice made from frozen water.

在電影中，有幾種版本的刨冰用於傳達，在以前的時代更具懷舊的感受，不論是在場景中，男女主角擦出愛的火花，或是一個慈愛的父親，在離家許久後，帶了刨冰回家給孩子們。很多現代版的刨冰在製作時確實有加入牛奶，但傳統的做法僅僅是水做的冰而已。

1 北台灣的文化風情

2 中台灣的魅力風情

3 南台灣的熱力風情

4 東台灣農村風情

Q2 Why are red beans considered an ingredient for dessert in Taiwan?
為何紅豆在台灣會被用來當甜品？

A Actually, red beans are a popular dessert ingredient throughout East and South Asia – not only in Taiwan.

事實上，紅豆在整個東亞和南亞都是流行的甜點食材，不是只有在台灣而已。

B I'm not sure why. Perhaps it is because they are starchy, have that chewy texture that many Taiwanese people love, and are really high in important minerals like iron and magnesium.

我不知道為什麼。也許是因為紅豆有澱粉成份，吃起來有嚼勁的口感，許多台灣人就喜歡這種口感，紅豆真的也含有高度重要的礦物質如鐵質與鎂。

C When they are cooked in sugar water, they are as sweet as fruit, and perhaps easier to keep on the shelf.

紅豆放入糖水煮時，吃起來就甜得像水果一樣，也許有加糖的紅豆更容易保持長久。

1 北台灣的文化風情

2 中台灣的魅力風情

3 南台灣的熱力風情

4 東台灣農村風情

Q3 Are these large shaved ice mountain servings meant to be shared with a friend?

這麼大一碗的刨冰主要是可以跟朋友一起分享的嗎？

A I suppose you could share, but since so much of the serving is ice, it's not really very filling.

我想是可以與朋友一起分享的，份量看起來這麼多，但其實不是真的很有飽足感。

B Sure, of course you can – then you can have room to try something else.

當然可以分享，這樣肚子才會有空間吃別的。

C For me, it depends on what flavor. I love mango shaved ice so much that I am not very good at sharing my dish.

對我來說，要看是什麼口味的。我很喜歡芒果刨冰，我不會分享我的冰。

Information 美食報馬仔

比起西式冰淇淋，台式的冰其實比較適合炎熱天氣的消暑甜品。楊吉利冰果室位在桃園區民族路，愛玉、杏仁凍、鳳梨醬與酸梅醬等都很台味。中壢市中山路的隆發冰果室也被稱呼為「榕樹下阿嬤古早冰」，主要品項是古早味的新鮮綿綿冰。加香蕉水的清冰加煉乳是道地的古早味。當地人都知道，桃園區中正路和三民路的小夜城冰果室、冰菓小夜城、小夜城冰菓都是同一家。有現打果汁、古早味剉冰和水果切盤。

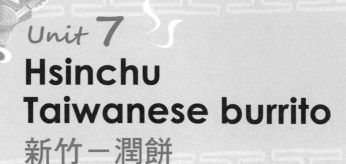

Unit 7
Hsinchu
Taiwanese burrito
新竹－潤餅

 ## Attractions 景點報報

　　新竹玻璃工藝博物館離新竹車站步行 15 分鐘，博物館是日治時代所建，有廣大的戶外空間休閒空間。後面是新竹市立動物園及夜市。新竹城隍廟是台灣最大的城隍廟，新竹城隍廟小吃市集有很多手工特製的新竹特產炒米粉、貢丸湯、肉圓的傳統美食，也有受歡迎的潤餅、肉燥飯、魷魚羹及冬瓜茶。新竹縣到處可以吃得到傳統客家菜，如醃製品、粄條、薑絲大腸、客家小炒和梅干扣肉。

 ## Popular snacks / street food 人氣小吃報報

Taiwanese burrito, like their cousins the fried egg rolls and Vietnamese fresh summer rolls, consists mainly of thin, cooked stretchy wheat-based wrappers encasing meat and vegetables into a neat cylindrical package. Typically, you will find a marinated pork mixture, or possibly tofu and eggs, as the protein plus vegetables like cabbage, carrots, bean sprouts, shitake mushrooms, celery, and cilantro. Peanut powder and sugar are a traditional topping just before the cook rolls the fillings into the wrapper.

Traditionally many families in Taiwan make them on Chingming Festival (Tomb-Sweeping Day). Since this dish can be a whole meal, on Chingming Festival, it can be made ahead of time so time is saved to visit the tombs of their family members to clean them, pull weeds, and to pray for their ancestors. People like this dish so much that you can find Taiwanese spring rolls in street markets morning or night. In Hsinchu, Family Guo's Taiwanese burrito is a famous vendor of this dish. Family Guo's has been selling Taiwanese burrito for more than a hundred years. They sell more than a thousand of them every night.

 中譯

　　潤餅的材料很像炸春卷或越南卷，潤餅主要是用很薄有咬勁的皮包裹肉和蔬菜捲成圓柱形方便用。潤餅內的食材通常是切絲煮過醃製豬肉、豆腐和蛋皮、再加蔬菜，如白菜、胡蘿蔔、豆芽、香菇、芹菜和香菜。潤餅在捲起來前會撒上花生粉和糖。在台灣很多家庭在清明節時也會自己做。這道菜本身吃起來算是一餐，在清明節時可以現做起來，剩餘的時間就用來掃墓、清雜草和祭拜祖先。大家都很喜歡這個小吃所以現在不管在白天市場或晚上夜市都可以買得的。在新竹城隍廟裡潤餅名聲最響亮的就是百年的「郭家潤餅」。這間從日據時代就在廟口旁擺攤到現在已經超過百年的歷史，聽說每天都可以賣到上千捲的潤餅。

1 北台灣的文化風情

2 中台灣的魅力風情

3 南台灣的熱力風情

4 東台灣農村風情

Q & A 外國人都是這樣問))) *MP3 07*

Q1 **How does the cook make the wrapper?**
潤餅皮是怎麼做的呢？

A Cooks at home normally buy pre-packaged wrappers. It's so much easier! On regular days, people don't wanna make Taiwanese burrito. People only make them at home when it is Chingming Festival. During that time, lots of vendors on the street will sell their made-on-the-spot wrapper.

一般在家做潤餅都是買做好的潤餅皮。這是很方便的。一般人平時不會在家自己做潤餅，通常只有在清明節時才會自己做。那段時間，路上就有很多攤販會現場做潤餅皮現場賣。

B The vendor makes a special wheat dough that he then wipes or rubs onto a hot, circular griddle. The ball leaves a thin layer behind on the pan. It cooks very quickly and is so fresh and delicious.

攤販會用發好的麵團，手拿著麵團在熱熱的大圓型鐵鍋上抹一圈，就會產生一層薄皮。做潤餅皮的過程很快，很新鮮很好吃。

60

C My neighbor used to make them and sell them in front of their house when it was close to Chingming Festival. The ingredients are only water, flour and salt. It is a very wet dough. Once it is mixed, leave it in the refrigerator overnight for it to slowly develop gluten.

我的鄰居以前常在接近清明節的時候在他們家前面擺一攤現做潤餅皮。我知道材料只有、水、麵粉與鹽。這是很濕的麵團。混合後放在冰箱長期發酵就會產生麵筋。

1 北台灣的文化風情

2 中台灣的魅力風情

3 南台灣的熱力風情

4 東台灣農村風情

Q2 **I love the cilantro in the Taiwanese burrito. Is cilantro often locally grown?**
我很喜歡潤餅裡面的香菜。香菜都是當地種的嗎？

A I love cilantro. Yes. It is often used for topping. I supposed it is mostly locally grown. It is a very cheap veggie.

But when you buy a bunch of vegetables from a vegetable vendor in a traditional market, the vendor usually gives you a small bunch of cilantro or green onion for free as a thank you gesture for your business.

我很喜歡香菜。是的，我們常常把香菜灑在菜上面。我想應該是當地種的，這是很便宜的菜。

但是你去傳統市場買菜，你一次買很多時，賣菜的人通常會送你一把香菜或蔥，當作謝謝你來照顧他的生意。

B I think so. The cilantro we have in Taiwan has a stronger flavor than the common Italian cilantro in the US.

我想應該是。台灣香菜的味道比一般在美國流行的義大利香菜味道還要香。

C Unfortunately, I don't like cilantro. My father used to run a Chinese herbal shop. He said cilantro has no significant nutrition and pesticides are not washed away completely.

很不幸的是，我不喜歡香菜。我爸爸以前開一家中藥行，他說香菜是沒有什麼營養，而且農藥常常存留在香菜上很難完全洗掉。

Q3 What are your favorite fillings for Taiwanese burrito?

你最喜歡潤餅裡加什麼料？

A I like all the fillings, and I especially love the combination of the cilantro and the peanut powder on top of everything.

我都很喜歡，我特別喜歡香菜與花生粉加在一起的味道。

B The more colorful the better for me, so spicy pork, carrots, purple cabbage, and anything else pretty.

我喜歡看起來很多顏色的潤餅、醃過的豬肉、 紅蘿蔔、紫色高麗菜，以及所有漂亮顏色的材料我都喜歡。

C I really prefer the vegetarian versions with tofu, lots of dried radish, bean sprouts, cabbage and carrots.

我會比較喜歡素食的潤餅加很多的豆腐、菜脯、豆干、豆芽菜、高麗菜和紅蘿蔔⋯等。

Information 美食報馬仔

　　新竹城隍廟的柳家滷肉飯、林家肉圓、王記蚵仔煎、阿城號炒米粉都是網友強力推薦的小吃。郭潤餅店餡料扎實的潤餅，常常大排長龍，是新竹城隍廟小吃的代表之一。鄭家魚丸燕圓是當天手工用新鮮魚漿現做，粉紅色的燕丸是因為加了紅糟，連家阿婆的米粉貢丸也是不能錯過。百年老店「阿城號」據說是城隍廟小吃的第一攤，包餡大貢丸、炒米粉、貢丸湯、肉圓等都是「阿城號」的人氣小吃。

1 北台灣的文化風情

2 中台灣的魅力風情

3 南台灣的熱力風情

4 東台灣農村風情

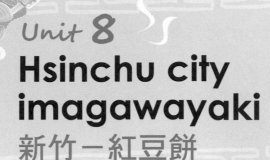

Unit 8
Hsinchu city imagawayaki
新竹－紅豆餅

 Attractions 景點報報

新竹市沿海有海八景觀光帶景點，十八尖山是由十八個峰頭組成的丘陵地帶，這裡的正一公園是登山健行的好去處。十九公頃青青草有櫻花、楓林、油桐步道是健走的好地方。從新竹火車站就可搭乘火車到內灣車站逛內灣老街，內灣老街總長約有 200 公尺，街道兩都是具有地方特色的野薑花肉粽、紫玉菜包、客家擂茶、擂茶冰沙、牛浣水、過鍋米粉、客家麻糬等美食。

 Popular snacks / street food 人氣小吃報報

Japanese's rule over Taiwan from 1895 to 1945 influenced the island's appearance as well as its cuisine. Japan sought to make Taiwan a model colony and produced an economy that would further aid its expansionist plans. So, Japan poured many resources into the island, modernizing roads, rail, energy, and helping to boost Taiwan into the industrial powerhouse it is today. Imagawayaki (red bean pastry) is a traditional dessert dating from Japan's 18th century that is still a welcome by-product of Japan's colonization of Taiwan. It is essentially pancake batter, cooked in a special griddle that looks like a giant western muffin tin or open waffle iron with round holes instead of square holes. As the batter begins to cook, the vendor adds a large spoonful of filling on top of the batter. The most traditional type is red bean paste, though more street market stalls are also selling custard, peanut, Asian cabbage, dried turnip, and curry-filled imagawayaki. "Zhu Cheng Red Bean Pastry" is a famous place for red bean pastry in northern Hsinchu City. They sell red bean pastry with a variety of fillings such as red bean, cream butter, taro paste, sesame, dried radish and cabbage.

 中譯

　　日本從 1895 年到 1945 年 統治台灣也同時影響了台灣的飲食。日本有心要把台灣建立為一個模範 殖民地以進一步的邁向日本擴張領土的目的。所以日本在台灣這個島嶼上投入了很多的資源，改建道路、鐵路、能源設施，這些後來都是幫助台灣走向工業轉型的重要背景。「紅豆餅」也就是車輪餅是一個傳統的甜點，其歷史可以追溯到日本的 18 世紀，這個小吃現在在台灣仍然很受歡迎。基本上是把麵糊倒入特殊的鐵鑄模烘烤，模子看起來像一個巨大的西式鬆餅烤具或是開放式有鐵圓孔的鬆餅，而不是一般的方型孔。麵糊煎熟後中央再填入餡，再取兩片餅皮夾合就完成。竹城紅豆餅在新竹市很受歡迎，賣的內餡有奶油，花生，最近幾年還有鹹味的紅豆餅，內餡高麗菜，蘿蔔乾甚至有咖哩內餡。賣的口味有：紅豆、奶油、芋頭、芝麻、菜脯和高麗菜。

Q & A 外國人都是這樣問))) *MP3 08*

Q1 **How does the cook get the filling inside the pancake?**
紅豆餅是如何把內餡加到裡面的呢？

Ⓐ He actually cooks two halves of the imagawayaki at the same time but in separate holes of the griddle, placing the filling on top of one half as it cooks.

Then when the batter gets firm on the bottom, he picks up the half without the filling and puts it on top of the filled half to finish cooking.

其實是同時在鐵鑄模的兩個孔中的麵皮牆，其中一個麵皮牆加入餡。

當底面煎熟了，把另一個麵皮牆蓋上有餡的麵皮牆。

Ⓑ You are looking for a hole in the side like jelly-filled doughnuts, but you won't find it. The vendor adds the filling as it cooks, not after.

你找填入內餡像甜甜圈那樣的洞，但是你是找不到的。攤販是在做紅豆餅時就加入內餡了，不是在之後。

C Let's watch the vendor make the next batch, if the people in the long line will let us get close enough. Would you like to get a cold drink first since the griddle puts off a lot of heat?

我們可以看看他們下一個要做的麵糊，如果排在前面的人可以讓我們靠近一點看的話就好。因為鐵鑄模很燙，你要靠近前要不要先買一瓶冷飲？

What are your favorite fillings for imagawayaki?

你喜歡紅豆餅的口味是什麼？

A I like the sweet ones. Red bean and cream custard are my favorite. Yam filling is one that surprised me the most. Mashed yam is a golden color so it looks so yummy. Yam is also sweet by itself with no seasoning necessary. Mashed yam is also very satisfying so just eating three can make it a full meal.

我喜歡甜的。紅豆餡和奶油餡都是我最喜歡的。但是我吃過最驚喜的口味是地瓜餡紅豆餅，金黃色地瓜泥賣相極佳，地瓜泥本身是自然鮮甜，無需加人工調味，吃起來很美味。番薯泥是飽足感的食材，我吃三個就覺得吃了一餐！

B I actually like the savory taste. I tried cream mixed with corn and it was very good. I also had cheese mixed with mochi. It was really unusual. There are fillings such as braised ground pork, tuna fish and even chicken nugget.

我喜歡鹹味的，我有吃過奶油玉米，很好吃。我也有吃過起士麻薯，那真的很特別。還有肉燥，鮪魚甚至是雞塊的內餡都很特別。

C When we visited a night market, there were so many foods. My friend pointed out the vendor making the red bean pastry but I was so full that I could not eat anything more. However, I love night markets in Taiwan. It is just full of fun.

我們去逛夜市，那裡有好多的食物。我的朋友指給我看賣紅豆餅的攤販，可是我那時真的好飽，什麼也吃不下了。總之，我很喜歡台灣的夜市，真的很好玩。

1 北台灣的文化風情

2 中台灣的魅力風情

3 南台灣的熱力風情

4 東台灣農村風情

Q3 Is this expensive, since there is a special griddle and so much labor involved in making them?

這種餅貴嗎？因為需要特別的紅豆餅機，也需要不少人力？

A They cost 5-20 NTD, depending on where you buy them. Does that seem expensive to you?

通常是一個台幣 5 到 20 元，看你在哪裡買的，這樣你覺得很貴嗎？

B Some local people think they are really expensive, but they are also pretty large for a dessert in Taiwan.

有些當地人會覺得很貴，但是這也算是份量不小的點心。

C Local people don't eat a lot of desserts because to many of them it seems like an expensive luxury. Usually visitors want to try everything though, and don't mind the cost.

當地人不會吃很多的甜點，有不少人還會覺得貴，通常遊客不會覺得貴，因為他們什麼都想吃吃看。

Information 美食報馬仔

新竹的紅豆餅或車輪餅是很多人喜歡的下午點心。紅豆、奶油、芝麻、抹茶、芋頭、高麗菜、菜脯都是很受歡迎的口味。風車紅豆餅在城隍廟附近，竹城紅豆餅在新竹市水田街，田園爆漿紅豆餅也是城隍廟的人氣小吃，總店在桃園中原大學附近。新竹清夜店的大伯創意紅豆餅有韓式泡菜、竹炭抹茶、檸檬乳酪、地瓜奶油、芋頭奶油口味，萬丹紅豆餅在新竹有很多分店，是已經成立 20 年的老字號。

Unit 9
Miaoli Crystal dumplings
苗栗－水晶餃

 Attractions 景點報報

苗栗的「仰天湖」就是向天湖，這是賽夏族「矮靈祭」的祭場。南庄鄉的「神仙谷」有原始森林，巨石、峽谷、峭壁與激流。苗栗市的「苗栗水上人家客家美食街」位在新苗街，這是以前的太平街，鄰近南苗三角公園，這裡是從苗栗到公館的必經之路。苗栗因以客家人居多，閩南料理有不少客家料理與的影響，客家炆爛肉就與爛肉飯很類似，蘿蔔乾、白斬土雞、酸菜炒肉絲其實都是客家經典小菜。

 Popular snacks / street food 人氣小吃報報

Crystal dumplings – also known as Hakka dumplings – are savory steamed dumplings with a unique transparent skin wrapped around shrimp, chopped pork belly, bamboo shoots, and sometimes other vegetables. The dough is prepared and handled carefully and steamed just the right length time so that the dumpling doesn't tear and lose its filling. Good crystal dumplings will be served fresh and hot, made in the appropriate size to pop the entire piece in the mouth at once. Miaoli City has the best crystal dumplings in Taiwan, thanks to the large percentage of Hakka living there. Miaoli County is one of two or three regions of Taiwan with a significant population of Hakka-speaking Han Chinese. Though Traditional Mandarin is the official language of Taiwan, the country values the many local dialects and indigenous languages of the island. The government of Taiwan is a global leader in studying and preserving the Hakka culture and language. It even sponsors Hakka news broadcasts, for example. "Sister A-Lan Crystal Dumpling" is a must-try in Miaoli City for Hakka crystal dumplings. The crystal dumplings with perfect chewy skin are made with ground pork mixed with celery, peppers and fried shallots.

 中譯

　　水晶餃是一種由獨特的透明外皮內包蝦，碎五花肉、竹筍和其他蔬菜的鹹蒸餃。水晶餃的皮要很小心地處理，且蒸的時間要剛好，這樣外皮才不會破裂，失去彈性。水晶餃最好是現煮現吃，水晶餃的大小是一口就可一次吃下。苗栗市有台灣最好吃的水晶餃，因為這裡有很多客家人。苗栗縣是台灣的客家語地區之一，這裡也有很多會講客語的閩南人。雖然中文是台灣的官方語言，但台灣很重視許多當地的方言和島上的原住民語言。台灣政府在研究和保存客家文化和語言是全球的領導者。比如，台灣政府甚至有贊助客家新聞廣播台。水上人家阿蘭姊水晶餃是在苗栗市一定要吃的客家水晶餃。完美外皮與嚼勁十足的水晶餃是必點小吃，內餡是豬肉拌入芹菜、胡椒以及油蔥酥。

1 北台灣的文化風情

2 中台灣的魅力風情

3 南台灣的熱力風情

4 東台灣農村風情

Q & A 外國人都是這樣問 ◎)) *MP3 09*

Q1 **How does the cook make the wrapper?**
水晶餃的皮是怎麼做的呢？

Ⓐ This is an interesting process of adding boiling water to sweet potato flour and manioc starch. I tried it before, but it took me three attempts to get it right. The first time I added too much water. The second time was a little better but the dough was still too wet. I finally got it right the third time. The boiling water has to be poured slowly into the flour mix.

這個做法很有趣，是地瓜粉與樹薯澱粉混合後加入熱水。我有做過但試到第三次才成功。第一次是水加太多。第二次比較好，但麵團還是太濕。後來我查了網路資料做研究也練習後，終於在第三次成功了。熱水要慢慢倒入麵粉中。

Ⓑ It is made with sweet potato flour and manioc starch. Hot water is added to the flour. No kneading required. There is no gluten in the dough, so it is easy to use hands to press it carefully into a circle before filling and steaming the dumpling.

76

那個皮是地瓜粉與樹薯澱粉混合後加入熱水，無需揉麵團。因為這種麵團沒有麵筋，所以很容易就可以用手輕輕的捏成圓形後包入內餡再炊熟。

C The hard part is not making the wrapper. It is pleating and pinching it around the filling. Because there is no gluten, the dough is not elastic and not easy to make pleats.

最難的不是皮的做法，最難的是捏出水晶皮上的皺摺。因為沒有麵筋，所以皮沒有彈性，也就不容易做出好看的皺摺。

Q2 What are some other Hakka influences found in the food of Taiwan?

有哪些台灣食物裡是有客家菜的影響？

A There are many foods in Taiwan with Hakka origins. One popular dish is called stuffed bean curd.

有很多台灣菜是受到客家菜的影響。有一道是釀豆腐。

B Sometimes it is just the flavorings or spices added to typical foods, such as using garlic instead of ginger for a soup.

有時候就只是調味料的不一樣。有時只是加薑絲或蔥末的不同。

C I love very much a Hakka tea called ground tea or pounded tea. It is made from assorted green tea leaves, plus sesame seeds, ground peanuts, mung beans, mint leaves and other herbs. Then just add water.

我很喜歡客家擂茶。這是將茶葉、芝麻、花生、米籽等食材，研磨後加開水就是可以。

Q3 **Is this different from the similar-looking dumplings I've had at Chinese buffets in the US?**

你覺得這個小吃跟我在美國的中國餐館所吃到的水餃是類似的嗎？

A Since I've not tried the crystal dumplings in your country, I don't know. Let's sample some and you tell me if it tastes differently.

我沒有吃過你國家的水晶餃，我不知道。我們就在這裡吃吃看，你可以告訴我是否吃起來有何不同？

B That depends on the expertise of your local chef, but sometimes a careless dim sum chef might just put only a lot of shrimp inside. Adding pork belly fat is what makes this one so juicy.

就看做的師傅是怎麼做的。有時做得比較粗糙的就放很多蝦，沒有豬肥肉在裏面，這樣吃起來就沒有汁。

C Usually crystal dumplings are cooked and served right away. It would be difficult to keep crystal dumplings in perfect condition as they sit on a hot buffet table waiting to be chosen by a diner. It is probably not that good to eat.

通常水晶餃都是現煮現吃的。自助餐式的水晶餃都一直在保溫狀態，應該不會好吃。

 ## *Information* 美食報馬仔

　　水上人家的阿蘭姊水晶餃已經是 50 年的老店，超 Q 外皮的水晶餃是這必點小吃，水上人家的鴨血湯是苗栗之最，鴨血是有經過油炸，這樣的鴨肉吃起來有點硬有點乾，很特別。這是來到水上人家必點的菜。「江記餛飩」緊鄰水上人家，有此一說「來苗栗如果沒吃過江記的餛飩與肉圓，以及水上人家的鴨血，就不算來過苗栗」。

北台灣的文化風情 1

中台灣的魅力風情 2

南台灣的熱力風情 3

東台灣農村風情 4

Unit 10 Miaoli Stinky Tofu 苗栗－臭豆腐

Attractions 景點報報

清安豆腐街前身是苗栗泰安鄉清安村洗水坑老街。清安以前是叫洗水坑。客家話清水就是「洗水」，是冬瓜山的一條乾淨清澈的洗水溪。身處豆腐街可以感受濃濃客家山城的氣息，這條街兩旁有木造建築，商店販賣的都是一些客家傳統小食，這裡主打的是好山好水做出來的豆腐，很多賣豆腐料理的店。「鷂婆山休閒步道」位於豆腐老街入口前，客家話的「鷂婆」是老鷹的意思。

Popular snacks / street food 人氣小吃報報

Stinky tofu is perhaps the most notorious street food in Taiwan, due to its strong, distinctive odor. The “Blue Cheese of Taiwan” is one of its nicknames. Essentially, this treat consists of soybean curd (AKA tofu), marinated in fermented brine and served deep-fried, stewed in a spicy soup base, steamed soft and used as a condiment, or barbecued. Stinky tofu and fermented tofu are similarly made. One popular story about how fermented tofu was invented recounts a young Qing dynasty (1644 to 1912) student, failing the imperial examination. He decided to open his own shop in the city and wait there until the next exam was administered. During one hot summer, Zhihe became worried about the shelf life of his tofu, so he tried to preserve it in a salty sauce. After a few days he checked on the tofu in the clay jar and found its odor nearly overwhelming. This could be the inspiration for fermented tofu. In Miaoli, Taiwan, there is a street called "Qing An Tofu Street." Visitors can taste many unique tofu dishes such as fried black bean curd, tofu salad, tofu medicine stew, fried white tofu, fried tofu and fried tofu balls.

 中譯

　　臭豆腐因為有強烈、獨特的氣味,也許最惡名昭彰的台灣小吃。「台灣藍起司」是其中一個綽號。基本上,臭豆腐是將豆腐醃泡在鹽水中裡發酵,可以炸,放在辣湯裡燉,可以蒸軟,甚至可以用來做調味品或燒烤。發明臭豆腐的其中一個說法是清朝(1644 年至 1912 年)的年輕人上京考試,因為沒有考上科舉,他決定在城市裡開一家自己的店,同時可以準備下一次的考試科舉。在一個炎熱的夏天,他開始擔心豆腐的保質期,所以把豆腐放在鹹醬裡。幾天後,他查看醬缸裡的豆腐後發現氣味幾乎讓人難以忍受。這可能是發酵豆腐的前身。在苗栗清安豆腐街可以吃到很多的豆腐料理如炸黑豆腐、涼拌豆腐、藥燉豆腐湯、炸白豆腐、煎豆腐和炸豆腐丸子。

1 北台灣的文化風情

2 中台灣的魅力風情

3 南台灣的熱力風情

4 東台灣農村風情

Q1 What is included in the stinky tofu brine?
醃製臭豆腐水裡面的料是什麼？

A Tofu cooks keep this information very secret. I doubt we can ever find out for certain.

做臭豆腐的師傅對這些資料是非常保密的。我懷疑我們不一定問的出來。

B Stinky tofu brine can include fermented milk, vegetables, and meat, dried shrimp, greens, bamboo shoots, and various herbs. All of these are fermented together prior to adding the tofu.

臭豆腐醃製包括發酵乳、蔬菜、肉、蝦米、青菜、竹筍以及各種草藥。在加入豆腐之前，這些所有的材料是先混在一起先發酵的。

C The cook soaks the tofu squares in a fermented brine of milk, vegetables, meat, fish, and herbs. Its odor is not only strong, but reminds me of pig manure. Oh, my goodness!

臭豆腐的師傅會把豆腐塊泡在有牛奶，蔬菜，肉，魚，和草藥水的發酵液體。這種氣味不僅很強，會讓我想到豬糞。我的天啊！

1 北台灣的文化風情

2 中台灣的魅力風情

3 南台灣的熱力風情

4 東台灣農村風情

Q2 Do people cook with stinky tofu at home?
會有人自己在家做臭豆腐嗎？

A My mom buys fermented stinky tofu from the market. She pan fries raw stinky tofu until it is golden outside. In another pot she heats up soy sauce, rock sugar and water and cooks it until thickened. Then she adds stinky tofu to the sauce.

我媽媽會在市場買臭豆腐。她的做法是把臭豆腐煎至兩面焦黃。在另外一鍋放入老醬油，冰糖粉和水煮成濃稠醬汁。再把臭豆腐放入醬汁一起煮。

B Stinky tofu can be steamed. Add Chinese sauerkraut, soybeans, mushrooms, hot peppers, cilantro, sesame oil, black vinegar, salt, soy sauce, and sugar. Steam it for 10 minutes. Before serving, garnish with chopped cilantro on top.

可以做清蒸臭豆腐，加酸菜、毛豆、香菇、紅辣椒、麻油、黑醋、鹽、醬油、糖各適量。中火蒸約十分鐘後要吃前撒上碎芫荽即成。

C My mother never bought it and cooked it at home. I think it is a mainlander dish to her so she never buys it. We always eat it in the night market. The stinky tofu vendor in my hometown night market has the best stinky tofu.

我媽媽從來沒有買臭豆腐在家自己煮過。我想對她來說這是外省菜，所以她不會想到要買回家自己煮。我們會在夜市買來吃。我家附近夜市賣的臭豆腐是最好吃的。

Q3 What is your favorite way to eat stinky tofu?
你最喜歡吃臭豆腐的方法是什麼呢？

A Because of the crispy outside, I love deep-fried tofu, dipped in a sweet-and-sour sauce. It goes well with pickled cabbage.

我喜歡吃炸臭豆腐，因為脆脆的外皮，加上甜甜酸酸的醬，配上泡菜口感就很清爽。

B Barbecued stinky tofu is my favorite. It is slightly deep fried. Several cubes of the fermented tofu are skewered on a stick, then gently barbecued over charcoal with plenty of spices. This process masks the strong odor of the tofu itself. Some pickled vegetables are added on the top.

炭烤臭豆腐是我的最愛。先短暫油炸後，串起來再用炭火慢慢炭烤，烤的時候還會加上醬汁，這樣的過程可以掩蓋豆腐的臭味，加上自家醃製的泡菜就很棒。

C Actually, I don't like stinky tofu. The smell is just too much. I visited a street called Tofu Street. I had the deep fried black tofu. This is first time I heard of black tofu. It is made with black beans. It does not have fermentation so it does not have a stinky smell. We also had Hakka bamboo shoot soup. The soup has bamboo shoots and Fu veggie which is fermented mustard greens that is a specialty only found in Hakka cooking.

我其實不喜歡臭豆腐。那種味道太強了。我有去過苗栗的豆腐街，我有吃炸黑豆腐，那很令人驚奇。灑上胡椒粉真的很特別。這是我第一次聽到有黑豆腐這道菜。這是用黑豆所做的黑色豆腐，是沒有發酵過的，所以沒有臭味。我們還喝了客家筍湯，湯裡有竹筍和福菜。福菜是發酵過的芥菜，是客家料理很獨特的材料。

Information 美食報馬仔

　　苗栗苑裡有好幾家有名的臭豆腐，「苑裡臭豆腐」就在苗栗縣苑裡鎮天下路消防隊旁邊。苑裡臭豆腐常常高朋滿座，外酥內嫩的臭豆腐加上酸泡菜讓很多人回味無窮。苑裡臭豆腐也賣餛飩湯，餛飩麵，豬血湯，乾麵與陽春麵，還有較少見的炸餛飩。天下路與建國路交叉口有家古早味鵝肉攤店，也有賣脆皮炸豆腐與炸餛飩，也是在地人的美食。

1 北台灣的文化風情

2 中台灣的魅力風情

3 南台灣的熱力風情

4 東台灣農村風情

Part 2

中台灣的魅力風情

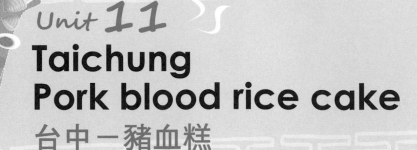

Unit 11
Taichung
Pork blood rice cake
台中－豬血糕

 ## *Attractions* 景點報報

台中火車站前有許多公車可以到國立自然科學博物館、植物園、文化中心、國立台灣美術館與美術園道,美術園道是一條綠意盎然很長的公園步道,也設計有小朋友可以玩的圓形廣場,在美術園道的盡頭就是國立台中美術館。精明一街有很多露天咖啡座,整體氣氛很優雅,是過個浪漫夜晚的好地方。熱鬧非凡的逢甲夜市是台中最具人氣的商圈。

 ## *Popular snacks / street food* 人氣小吃報報

Pig's blood rice cake is served on a stick in many night markets in Taiwan. The name is perhaps a little too honest for some, but the ingredients and texture are not completely unfamiliar to anyone who eats sausage, especially traditional European forms like boudin from France. Firm, yet chewy is the best way to describe the texture. This treat on a stick is made from sticky rice cooked in pork blood. Once firm, the warm cake is usually dipped in a soy-pork broth or sweet and sour sauce and rolled in cilantro and sweet peanut powder. The origins of such a dish likely date back to old days when farmers did not want to waste the blood that drained from ducks that they had slaughtered. Duck meat and blood are valuable in Chinese medicine, so making a rice cake from the duck blood was not only frugal, but also healthy. Visitors to Taichung City can enjoy the best pig's blood rice cake at Fengjia Night Market in Taichung County. This night market is the second largest in Taiwan.

 中譯

　　串在竹籤上的豬血糕在很多台灣夜市都有賣。這個名字也許太真實了一點，但它的成分和質感對於吃香腸的人來説並不是完全陌生，特別是歐洲傳統的香腸，如來自法國的 boudin。口感扎實也有嚼勁是很多人描述吃豬血糕的感覺。豬血糕由糯米加豬血所煮成的。一旦蒸熟成型後，熱熱的豬血糕通常沾醬吃或裹上香菜和花生粉。這個小吃的起源可能要追溯到以前農民不想浪費他們宰殺的鴨子所排出的血液。鴨肉和血在中藥裡是很有價值的，所以用鴨血所做的豬血糕不僅節儉，而且還健康。隨著時間的轉換，與豬肉比起來鴨肉變得更加昂貴，所以豬血就取代鴨血來做豬血糕。遊客可以在台中的逢甲夜市吃到最好的豬血糕。逢甲夜市是台灣第二大夜市。

Q1 Is this the only way to eat pig's blood rice cake, coated with peanut powder and chopped cilantro?

在夜市我有看到人家吃豬血糕裹滿花生粉及香菜，這是豬血糕唯一的吃法嗎？

Ⓐ No. Pig's blood rice cake can be boiled with broth, steamed, braised, deep fried, stir fried and etc. There are regional style differences as well. In the south, pig's blood rice cake is coated with sweet and sour sauce, soy sauce paste or with ginger. In the north, pig's blood rice cake is coated with peanut powder and some cilantro.

不止。有很多方法可以吃豬血糕，可以煮湯、蒸、滷、炸、炒等。每個地方的吃法也不一樣。南部吃法是加甜辣醬、醬油膏、薑絲，而北部吃法是裹上花生粉及少量香菜。

Ⓑ Pig's blood rice cake is one of several items at a Taiwanese style chicken nugget vendor. After pig's blood rice cake and other items are chosen, the vendor will cut pig's blood rice cake into square pieces and deep fry it. Black peppers, white peppers and hot pepper mix are added.

台灣鹽酥雞的攤位很多都有豬血糕，顧客選好豬血糕和其他食物後，攤販會把豬血糕切塊後丟入油鍋炸，然後撒上黑胡椒粉、白胡椒粉和辣粉。

C Pig's blood rice cake is also popular among hot pot ingredients. It also can be added to sesame oil chicken soup or ginger duck soup. The rice cake will soak in the fat in the soup.

豬血糕也可以放入火鍋料、麻油雞或薑母鴨的湯中，豬血糕會吸收湯汁的油脂。

A Pig's blood rice cake is my favorite. After the rice cake is steamed, it is coated with soy sauce paste, peanut power and cilantro.

我的最愛是豬血糕。剛蒸出來的米血刷上醬油膏，裹上一層花生粉，最後再灑上香菜。

B Minglun Pancake is my first choice. The sign says "pancake" but it is much more like French crepe. The vendor pours a scoop of pre-mixed flour and water on to the iron pan then presses the batter out to be as thin as possible. Green onions and eggs are added. Sweet and sour sauce is added then the pancake is rolled up and ready to serve. It is already 10 o'clock here at Fengjia Night Market, but there are people everywhere eating and buying. The Taiwanese lifestyle is inseparable from night markets.

明倫蛋餅是我的第一選擇。說是美式煎餅，但其實比較像法式的煎餅。老闆在煎台上煎餅皮，灑蔥花、打上蛋，加上獨家的甜辣醬後淋上醬料捲起來。十點多的逢甲夜市人還很多，逛夜市真的覺得台灣人已經離不開夜市了。

C Rice sausage with Taiwanese pork sausage in the middle was my favorite. I loved to top it with raw garlic and sour greens. My Hakka friend told me that this dish was invented by Hakka in Hualien. It is satisfying and easy for workers to pack for their lunch.

大腸包小腸是我的最愛，那是切開烤過的糯米腸，夾住烤過的台式香腸，塗上醬油膏等醬料，用炭火或爐火烤熟後，加上生大蒜及酸菜即成。我的客家朋友跟我說大腸包小腸是以前台灣花蓮客家人發明的，是出門工作方便攜帶又能飽食的午餐。

1 北台灣的文化風情

2 中台灣的魅力風情

3 南台灣的熱力風情

4 東台灣農村風情

Q3 Is it safe to eat a dish made with pig's blood?
用豬血做的東西吃的安心嗎？

A This is not raw blood. It's cooked, as you can tell from the color. It is strange but it is edible.

這不是生血，是有煮熟的，因為你可以從顏色看出來。豬血這種材料是很奇怪但是可以吃的。

B It is very common in traditional European cooking. Pig's blood is a traditional ingredient in popular European dishes like blood pudding and blood sausage, plus it is used to thicken the popular French dish Coq au Vin (COKE-o-VAN).

這個在傳統歐洲烹飪是非常普遍的。豬血是一個傳統的食材，如歐洲流行菜餚裡的血布丁或血腸，豬血也可以用來做紅酒燉雞。

C Some compare pig's blood dish to Korean Soondae – a blood sausage in a casing that is also often served on a stick.

有人把這道豬血糕與韓國的 Soondae 做比較，這是一種血腸也可以用竹子串起來吃。

 ***Information* 美食報馬仔**

··

在逢甲夜市必吃的就是日船章魚燒。帝鈞胡椒餅也是排隊美食，胡椒餅是用料扎實的豬肉內餡，濃餅皮散發出來的胡椒香味真的讓人吃得很滿足。很多人會推薦士林爆醬雞排還有逢甲夜市的大腸包小腸，逢甲茶葉蛋是逢甲夜市著名的小吃之一，在逢甲是老店。「四方烤鴨夾餅」以烤鴨夾餅聞名。台北豬血糕，一心素食臭豆腐也都是遠近馳名！

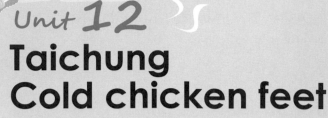

Unit 12
Taichung
Cold chicken feet
東海－雞腳凍

Attractions 景點報報

　　東海大學校地廣大、大樹林立，是散步的好地方，校內的路思義教堂是台灣建築指標之一。東海大學鄰近景點有東海古堡，是日據時代的軍事碉堡。望高寮是台中地區最看夜景最棒的地方。東海藝術街商圈多為古董、茶坊及咖啡店等特色店家，也被稱為東海國際藝術街。東海夜市在東海大學後方是很多美食的集中地，弘光科技大學及靜宜大學等學校都在附近。

Popular snacks / street food 人氣小吃報報

Cold chicken feet. While the name may not be appealing to some western tastes, chicken feet are an important part of traditional cuisines all over the world. Nowhere are chicken feet more popular than Taiwan, Hong Kong, and China. In fact, poultry producers in the United States make significant profits exporting chicken feet to Asia. Over the past 20 years, occasional poultry import bans due to faltering trade agreement negotiations or fears of avian flu have restricted the flow of US chicken to Asia.

Typically, when added together, Taiwan, Hong Kong, and China are the destination of almost 25 percent of the US' poultry exports – an indication of how important chicken feet really are in the culture. Chicken feet are a traditional dim sum treat, originating in the Cantonese region of China, making them a perfect dish to enjoy from a street vendor in Taiwan. In night markets in Taiwan, especially the most famous place to buy them in Taichung City, they are served cold. It's not normally a hot and spicy dish, instead relying on the richness of the gelatinous texture of the feet, the skin, and the cooking process.

 中譯

　　雞腳凍。雖然這個名字可能不會吸引西方人的胃口，雞爪其實是世界各地傳統美食一個重要的食材。沒有其他地方的雞爪比台灣、香港和中國更受歡迎。事實上，美國家禽生產商出口到亞洲雞爪有獲得顯著的利潤。在過去的 20 年裡，有時因為搖擺不定的貿易協定談判或對禽流感的憂慮禁止家禽進口，而制約了美國雞肉在亞洲的流動。一般情況下，台灣、香港和中國的市場需求加起來占有美國禽肉出口 24％的量，這也顯示雞爪在這些文化裡的重要性。雞爪是廣式飲茶的小吃，原自於中國的廣東地區，後來成為台灣流行的美食。在台灣的夜市，最有名的雞腳凍是在台中的夜市，這是冷食的。雞腳凍通常不是辛辣的小吃，雞腳凍好吃的地方是在雞腳的凝膠質，這是雞腳的皮所滷出來的口感。

Q & A 外國人都是這樣問 🔊)) *MP3 12*

Q1 What kinds of spices and sauces are used in its preparation?
製作的材料是什麼香料與醬汁呢？

Ⓐ Rice wine, sugar, star anise, garlic, ginger, soy sauce, black bean sauce, oyster sauce, pepper-all the typical flavorings of Taiwan.

米酒、白糖、八角、大蒜、生薑、醬油、醬油、蠔油、胡椒粉，其實都是台灣烹飪典型的調味料。

Ⓑ Both the marinade and the braising sauce have different spices, and the longer the feet are in the sauce, the richer the flavor. I can taste soy sauce, sweetness, a little something from the sea, garlic, ginger, and the spices you may know as Chinese Five Spice.

醃料和滷汁有不同的材料，雞腳醃在醬料中時間越長會越有味道。我有吃出醬油味，也甜味、還有一些海味、大蒜，還有一點生薑的味道，還有五香。

C It is not hard to make. First, blanch chicken feet in boiled water. In a different pan, fry garlic, ginger, hot pepper and chicken feet drained from water for a few minutes then add soy sauce, cooking wine, rock sugar, five spices and water. Braise it for 1.5 hours until chicken feet are soft to eat.

那不難做。準備一鍋煮滾的熱水汆燙雞爪，汆燙的同時，用一炒鍋把蒜頭、薑片和辣椒下鍋炒香後，加入汆燙好的雞爪，並加入醬油、酒、冰糖、五香粉與水，用小火滷煮 1.5 小時以上，直到雞爪軟爛。

1 北台灣的文化風情

2 中台灣的魅力風情

3 南台灣的熱力風情

4 東台灣農村風情

Why is this dish popular in Taiwan?
為什麼這道小吃在台灣這麼受歡迎呢?

A It is just fun to eat it. I love it with beer.

就是好吃。我喜歡配啤酒一起吃。

B It is never a main dish. It is a snack. It is something people like to eat when they feel relaxed or have free time. Tourists traveling to Taichung fixate on the gelatinous texture of chicken feet at the food stand. People grab dozens of chicken feet in the bag, eating them right after purchasing. Even if gnawing them on the street is not that convenient, people seem to enjoy it.

這不是主餐。是屬於點心類。一般人通常在輕鬆情況下或有時間時才會吃的點心。觀光客到台中旅遊將目光都注視到食物攤販上的雞腳凍膠質層。人們抓了幾十個雞腳凍放入袋子裡,在購買後即刻品嘗。即使在大街上吃雞腳凍不太方便,人們似乎很享受。

C Taiwanese people love to gnaw on the bones and get every last piece of flesh off of them. Nobody is in a rush when they are at the night market. Cold chicken feet is the perfect snack for leisure time to sit chatting with friends and drinking a beer.

台灣人喜歡啃骨頭，也會把骨頭啃得乾乾淨淨。逛夜市的人都不太會趕時間。雞腳凍是閒暇時間與朋友坐下來一起聊天，喝啤酒配的完美點心。

Q3 **How does the person eating it manage the bones inside the feet?**
吃雞腳凍時要怎麼吃裡面的骨頭？

A Just chew carefully until you can spit them out. It usually takes practice to chew the skin then spit the bones out.

就慢慢地吃然後再把骨頭吐出來。這通常是要練習的。

B It's okay to break off one bit at a time and suck on the small piece until you spit the bones back into your hand and then place it on the edge of your dish.

也是可以剝斷一小段，然後吃一點點後把骨頭吐到你的手上後再放到盤子邊。

C I am never good at eating chicken feet, but I love the flavor with cloves, star anise, cinnamon and other spices. It is very pleasant. I just chew the skin as much as I can.

我不是很會吃雞腳，但是我很喜歡雞腳滷的丁香，八角，桂皮等香料的味道。我就只是儘量啃雞腳外面的皮。

 ## *Information* 美食報馬仔

　　東海蓮心冰雞爪凍油亮滑嫩，不油膩 QQ 的口感是有名的排隊美食。這裡還有"蓮心冰"也是人氣冰品，冰淇淋加上甜味的彎豆是夏日好冰品。雞爪凍的斜對面就是人氣名店的「豆子」。這家店主要賣的是芋圓、薯圓及仙草等等相關製品。就如台灣很多夜市一樣，逢甲夜市的美食小吃真是太多了，雞排堡、芋圓仙草凍、福洲包、東山鴨頭、雞腳凍、割包、章魚小丸子都各有特色。

1 北台灣的文化風情

2 中台灣的魅力風情

3 南台灣的熱力風情

4 東台灣農村風情

Unit 13
Changhua
Salty Mochi
彰化—鹹麻糬

 ## *Attractions* 景點報報

　　八卦山風景區是台灣八大名勝之一，風景區裡有古砲，也有健康步道，八卦山風景區有三個區域，分別是八卦山、百果山、松柏嶺。八卦山的『大佛風景區』是彰化的佛教觀光聖地。百果山遊憩系統的大樟公樹裡有 300 餘年的樹齡，百果山登山步道是健行的好去處。松柏嶺遊憩系統則有兩個行車道，一是全線在山林中的長青自行車道；另外一個是以鐵道概念設計的二水自行車道全長共 15 公里。

 ## *Popular snacks / street food* 人氣小吃報報

The Taiwanese enjoy so much the slightly sticky, chewy texture in food that they naturally have retained mochi from the period of Japanese occupation. Made mainly from glutinous rice flour, carefully blended and cooked to the proper consistency, mochi may be more commonly known outside of Taiwan as a sweet dessert. Here, it is also available as a salty, spicy, savory snack with favorite Taiwanese ingredients: pork, seafood, soy sauce, and more. Visitors to Changhua may purchase two types of mochi: pre-packaged as a souvenir for friends back home, or fresh mochi that must be eaten within two days. There is even a mochi museum in nearby Nantou City, run by one of Taiwan's large processed food companies, "Royal Family." Mochi is also popular in Japan. Japanese families make mochi the traditional way to celebrate the New Year, with laborious hand-pounding of the rice. They may also own automatic mochi making machines so they can enjoy the snack at home year-round. Dayuan Bakery located near Cheng Huang Temple in Changhua sells famous salty mochi. In addition to the famous salty mochi, it also makes turnip mochi, taro mochi and other sweet mochi.

 中譯

　　台灣人很喜歡麻糬,這是從日據時代流傳下來的,有黏牙又有咬勁的小吃。主要由糯米粉加水調配煮到適當的稠度,大部份的人知道這是一種甜點。但是麻糬也有鹹與辣的口味,在台灣鹹麻糬的內餡通常有豬肉、海鮮、醬油等。到彰化的遊客可以購買兩種類型的麻糬:包裝好的可以買回家送給朋友,或現做新鮮麻糬必須在兩天內食用。在南投還有一個台灣麻糬主題館,由一家台灣大型食品加工廠「皇族」經營。麻糬在日本也很受歡迎,日本家庭會以傳統方式用手搗杵來做麻糬慶祝新年。現在也有自動麻糬製作機,這樣全年都可以在家裡享受這個小吃。在城隍廟旁大元餅行知名的鹹麻糬。除了有名的鹹麻糬,還有蘿蔔酥,芋頭酥和其他甜味的麻糬。

1 北台灣的文化風情

2 中台灣的魅力風情

3 南台灣的熱力風情

4 東台灣農村風情

Q1 **What flavors of salty mochi are available?**
鹹麻糬有什麼口味呢？

A Every vendor has their specialty. Most vendors will have both meat-based salty mochi and vegetarian ones. I tried salty mochi with radish filling and taro filling.

每個賣家都有自己的專門口味。大多數會賣有肉的鹹麻糬和素鹹麻糬。我有試過蘿蔔酥、芋頭酥的鹹麻糬。

B What flavor do you like? There are many mochi vendors in Changhua where you can call ahead and they will hand-make custom flavors for you! You need to be careful not to buy too many at once. Mochi can normally stay fresh and soft for two days at room temperature. It is tasty when it is freshly made.

你喜歡什麼口味？彰化有很多賣麻糬的商家會接受電話訂購，也會做你想要的口味。要小心，不要一下子買太多。麻糬在室溫下可以保鮮二天。很多賣家都是現包的，剛捏好的新鮮麻糬很好

吃。

~~~~~~

C I never had salty mochi. I grew up eating only sweet mochi. I like mochi with peanut powder and crushed peanut fillings. The outside is coated with soy bean powder. It is very delicious.

我從來沒有吃過鹹麻糬。我只有吃過甜的麻糬。我喜歡麻糬加了花生粉跟碎花生顆粒包成的內餡，外皮灑滿黃豆粉。非常好吃。

Besides pounding the rice, what are the other processes for making the mochi dough?
除了要攪拌的步驟外，做麻糬的糯米糰還需要什麼呢？

A The rice flour is mixed with a small amount of cold water, and then boiling water. Mixing it together thoroughly makes a gluey ball that is then steamed for about 30 minutes. Take out the dough and put it into a mixing bowl, slowly add sugar and mix until stiff. The dough is ready to be used for mochi.

糯米粉加少許的冷水後再加入滾水，混合成米糰後再蒸 30 分鐘。蒸完後放入攪拌器，同時慢慢加入糖攪拌，攪拌成糊狀即可用來做麻糬。

B Actually, in modern times pounding the rice is mainly a ceremonial tradition. Today, mochi makers most likely are purchasing sweet rice flour to make mochi.

其實，現在有用到攪拌這個步驟通常是一種慶祝性的傳統。現在做麻糬的都是買現成的糯米粉來做。

🅒 Dough made with sweet rice flour is actually very sticky. It's hard to handle. Recipes often say to lightly cover your hand with corn starch and lightly dust corn starch on the cooked sweet rice dough before working with the dough. Once a mochi is made, you can shake it gently to get some corn starch off.

糯米粉是很黏的，很難操做。食譜都會說要手沾玉米粉，做麻糬前的熟糯米團也要沾上玉米粉。麻糬做好後可以輕輕的晃一下把王米粉刷掉。

Q3 Are there traditional Taiwanese influences on mochi?

就麻糬來说是否有台灣傳統的影響？

A Several aboriginal tribes make a very similar dish to the sweet mochi that originated from Japan, only the tribes don't use rice flour, but instead use millet flour – a common grain in aboriginal cuisine.

有一些原住民部落的麻糬與源自日本的麻糬很類似，只是原住民部落是不用糯米粉，而是用小米，這是原住民美食常用到的食材。

B Yes, the Amis tribe living on the east coast in Hualien is especially famous for its own mochi, though not exactly like this rice mochi.

有的，在花蓮東海岸的阿美族部落做的麻糬特別有名，這與一般用糯米粉做的麻糬不一樣。

C Since Japanese mochi has been in Taiwan for over a hundred years and since similar dishes have long been eaten all over Asia, I'm not really sure what was introduced and what was created or modified here. It's just delicious!

日本式的麻糬在台灣已有一百多年了，類似的小吃其實在亞洲各地很流行，我真的不知道是誰發明麻糬或是誰做創新。麻糬就是好吃！

 ## Information 美食報馬仔

　　彰化的名產是麻糬，每一家的麻糬皮與餡料都有自我獨特的風味。「玉瓏坊麻糬」在彰化市民族一街，「玉華珍餅行」在彰化市辭修路，「大元餅行」隱身在彰化市民生路小巷子城隍廟旁，「大元餅行」的鹹麻糬的鹹口味有蘿蔔酥、芋頭酥、口酥餅和脆餅。「丁師傅麻糬」位於民俗文化館旁有鹹麻糬。傳統手工麻糬都是不含防腐劑，最好現做現買現吃，通常在兩日內要食用完。

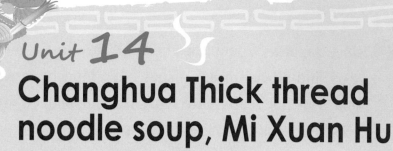

Unit 14
Changhua Thick thread noodle soup, Mi Xuan Hu
彰化－麵線糊

Attractions 景點報報

鹿港（LuKang）是一個小鎮，古蹟多廟也多。鹿港以前是天然良港，鹿港天后宮建立於 1725 年，是當地航海人的精神寄託，現是臺灣三級古蹟。龍山寺是國家一級古蹟，建於西元 1786 年建，佔地廣大，號稱台灣紫禁城，金門館館是廟宇也是金門同鄉會館。摸乳巷有 200 年的歷史，是狹窄的防火巷，巷長約 100 公尺，最窄處不到 70 公分。玉珍齋賣的是台灣古早味各式各樣的糕點。鹿港的菜市場裡就是鹿港美食中心。

Popular snacks / street food 人氣小吃報報

"Thread noodle soup with big intestines" is a must try in Taiwan. Oysters and large pig intestines are added to the basic noodle broth, then garnished with garlic and cilantro. The traditional way of making thread noodle by hand is a dying art. Even the weather has to cooperate in the process, since days that are too humid will cause the noodles to dry too slowly. In good weather, the process of making a batch of noodles still takes over 12 hours. The dough is a simple flour, water, salt mixture left to rest and ferment slightly before being stretched and pulled repeatedly, lengthening the fibers in the dough. The expert noodle-maker hangs a handful of stretchy dough on poles to allow gravity to help the process of thinning them as much as possible. Once the noodles have reached the proper thinness, the maker will hang them on a pole outside and do the one last stretch of the noodles – making them about one millimeter thick. Then the noodles are hung on poles in the sun to dry. "Mi Xuan Hu" is a variation of thick thread noodle soup only found in Changua where people have it for breakfast!!

 中譯

　　大腸麵線是在台灣一定要吃的美食。台灣人會把這個當午餐、午後點心或夜宵。高湯裡會加蚵仔和大腸燴，然後配上大蒜和香菜。傳統的麵線做法方式是快要消失的藝術。天氣是製造過程的元素之一，因為天氣太潮濕會導致麵條乾燥速度太慢。在天氣好的時候，製作一批麵線的過程中仍然需要 12 小時以上。麵團其實就是簡單的麵粉、水、鹽混合而已，靜置和發酵後再反復拉長麵團的纖維。麵線會被掛在空中，藉由地心引力使它長度盡可能的細化。麵線到了一定的長度後會放在戶外，最後一道功夫是做麵的人使出多年所學的力道把麵線拉出大約 1 毫米的薄度，麵線要掛在杆子上讓陽光曬乾。「麵線糊」是用麵線來做羹湯，這只有在彰化才有，只有彰化人拿來當早餐。

Q & A 外國人都是這樣問 🔘)) *MP3 14*

Q1 **Is there only one kind of thick thread noodle soup?**
麵線糊的種類只有一種嗎？

A No. There are three basic kinds. One is oyster thread noodle soup, one is big intestine thread noodle soup and the third is thick thread noodle soup. They are all similar. The soup is thick and thread noodles are used.

沒有，有三種基本的煮法。一種是蚵仔麵線，一種是大腸麵線，還有一種是麵線糊。他們其實都很類似，湯是濃稠，用的是也都是麵線。

B There are few varieties but the soup broth is similar which is a combination of traditional flavors: seafood, pork, garlic, onion, soy sauce, pepper. In southern Taiwan, the broth will be sweeter and perhaps also have more seafood than here in central Taiwan. In the north, the broth would be saltier.

是有很多種類但湯頭都很類似，就是傳統風味的組合：海鮮、豬肉、大蒜、蔥、醬油、胡椒粉。在台灣南部，湯汁會比較甜，或許也會比台灣中部加更多的海鮮。在北部，湯汁會比較鹹。

C In the south, I only know oyster thread noodle soup and big intestine thread noodle soup.

在南部，我只知道有蚵仔麵線和大腸麵線。

Have you ever made thread noodles at home?
你會在家自己做這樣的麵線嗎？

A No one makes thread noodles at home. It is easy to buy and it is cheap. My family just walks to the end of the street to buy from the thread noodle maker.

沒有人會在家裡自己做麵線。這很容易買到也很便宜。我家人走到街底就可以買到現做的麵線。

B No, I know a noodle maker in my home town, but it's much too difficult to try making the noodles this thin at home. This noodle only has flour, salt and water but it requires years of training, practice, and professional tools to make it. I heard that thread noodles made near the sea have a different taste than ones made in the country side. It has something to do with the wind coming from the sea.

我們家鄉就有人在做麵線。在家做這個難度太高。麵線的材料其實只有麵粉、水與鹽，但是要做好麵線需要多年的功夫也需要工

具。我還聽過在海邊附近做出來的麵線與在鄉下做出來的麵線不一樣。這與海風大有關。

C Not this type of noodle – that is a special process that requires years of apprenticeship. There are two types of thread noodles. One is white in color and must dry completely in the sun. The other kind is red thread noodles which are used for oyster thread noodle soup.

這種麵線不會有人在家自己做,這是需要多年的師徒學習才行。有兩種麵線分別是白麵線與紅麵線。蚵仔麵線裡用的就是紅麵線。

Q3 **What are these large chunks of seafood and these strange chewy rings on top of the soup?**
湯上面有大塊的海鮮還有怪怪的一圈圈的那是什麼？

A Oysters are in the soup. Don't forget that Taiwan is an island, so food from the sea is a necessary ingredient in many, many dishes. The rings are not squid like you might think – they are slices of pig intestines.

湯裡那是蚵仔，別忘了台灣是一個島嶼，所以很多料理有放來自海裡的材料是必然的。你看到的不是你想的魷魚，一圈圈的那是豬腸。

B There are oysters and also braised large pig intestines. Taiwanese love the taste, but especially the chewy texture of both! Don't worry about the intestines, they are thoroughly cleaned, soaked in salt water which helps kill the bacteria, and then braised for hours in spices, soy sauce, pork belly, onion, and ginger.

那是蚵仔還有滷過的豬腸。台灣人很喜歡這種味道，特別是有咬勁的材料。不用擔心腸子，那都有徹底清洗，浸泡在鹽水裡有助於殺滅細菌，然後用調味品、醬油、五花肉、蔥和薑燉上幾個小時。

C Aren't they good? Can you guess what they are? Oysters and large pig intestines. Yummy! After this, I dare you to try pig blood and thread noodle soup.

看起來很好吃對不對？你可以猜猜那是什麼呢？是蚵仔還有大腸。好吃！吃過這個，就看你敢不敢試試豬血湯麵線。

 ## Information 美食報馬仔

　　麵線糊是鹿港的在地傳統小吃更是很多鹿港人的傳統早餐。小小台灣光是麵線糊的做法就很不同，北港的麵線糊是白麵線，鹿港麵線是經過蒸過的紅麵線，「蔡麵線糊」、「王罔麵線糊」、「老林麵線糊」、「鹿港龍山麵線糊」都是在地人喜歡的麵線糊。在鹿港摸乳巷的附近的「俗擱大碗」的「無餓不坐麵線糊」20 多年來是當地人的最愛。

Unit 15
Nantou Noodles (yi mian)
南投－意麵

 Attractions 景點報報

　　南投猴探井風景區「天空之橋」是全台灣最長的天橋，長達 204 公尺，有 265 階，在橋上可以看到彰化與南投的景致。台灣麻糬主題館是食品公司的廠房，轉型後成為對外開放的觀光工廠。遊客可以體驗搗麻糬的樂趣，自己親手做的麻糬。草屯寶島時代村位於草鞋墩夜市旁，是一座以懷舊主題老台灣的文化創意園區，是很多人既熟悉又懷念的 50 年代的記憶。

 Popular snacks / street food 人氣小吃報報

Nantou, Taiwan's only landlocked county is famous for its yi mian. Some noodle makers sun dry yi mian in a big, flat bamboo basket. Dry yi mian can be kept longer. They look similar to what western consumers know as Ramen noodles. The noodle dough is unique because it traditionally includes duck egg white and soda water. Ducks were a main staple food in agricultural Taiwan. Duck yolks are soaked in salt for different dishes, leaving the whites as unneeded leftovers. Adding duck egg white to yi mian could be just a way to use all the leftover duck egg white. The soda water helps the noodles retain their spongy texture. Nantou County in Taiwan is 83% mountainous with 41 peaks reaching over 3,000 meters (9,800 feet) high. Beautiful inland lakes and ponds, like Sun Moon Lake, are popular tourist destinations. Nantou is also home to a 1500+ acre amusement park and cultural history living museum called Formosan Aboriginal Culture Village. The park celebrates eleven aboriginal tribes by recreating their villages and staging traditional performances for park attendees. Among the tribes featured is the smallest of Taiwan's recognized tribes, the Thao, who still make their home around Sun Moon Lake in Nantou.

　　南投，台灣唯一處於內陸的地方，以意麵最有名。這細扁的麵條通常都加在麵湯中。有些意麵也會在大竹籮上日曬至乾燥以利保存。乾意麵可以保存更久，意麵看起來很類似西方消費者所知道的速食麵。意麵的麵團跟一般做麵的麵團來説是比較獨特，因為意麵的麵團用的是鴨蛋蛋白和蘇打水。鴨子在以前的農業台灣算是主食。鴨蛋黃被醃製後用在不同的料理，剩下的鴨蛋白很可能是因此廢物利用拿來做意麵。蘇打水有助於麵條保留其 QQ 的口感。南投縣內有台灣83％的山地，有 41 個山峰達到 3000 多公尺（9800 英尺）。這裡有美麗的內陸湖泊和池塘，像日月潭就是熱門的旅遊地。南投也有一個有 1500 英畝大的九族文化村，這是結合遊樂園和文化歷史生活館的觀光地。透過重建他們的村莊和傳統表演，九族文化村裡保留有 11 個原住民的傳統。其中很有特色的部落邵族是台灣官方承認最小的部落，他們的世代祖先都住在南投日月潭。

Q1 Are yi mian considered a food for tough financial times like instant noodles are in the west?

意麵是經濟蕭條時在吃的小吃嗎？就像在西方的速食麵一樣嗎？

A Not at all. Yi mian is a common food. Everyone can afford it, whether rich or poor.

不是。意麵是平民美食。有錢沒錢都可以付得起的美食。

B These instant noodles are extremely popular in Taiwan also as a satisfying, hot convenience food. But noodle vendors are everywhere in Taiwan as well. So students can easily go to a noodle vendor and order affordable yi mian.

速食麵在台灣是非常受歡迎也是讓人吃得飽的方便熱食。但是在台灣到處都有麵攤。因此，學生們可以很容易的去麵攤吃他們付得起的麵。

C Yi mian vendors sell noodles for breakfast, lunch or dinner. My sister and I used to go to an indoor market to eat Yi mian after our piano lessons. Now we live in different parts of the world. We still miss it very much. We never associated yi mian as being poor people's food. It is cheap compared to McDonald's.

意麵是可以用來當早餐，午餐或晚餐。我姊姊和我以前會在上完鋼琴課後去菜市場內吃意麵。現在我們姐妹住在世界不同的地方，我們仍然十分懷念意麵。我們從來沒有認為意麵是沒錢的人在吃的。跟麥當勞相比，意麵很便宜。

Q2 Do you have a favorite way to prepare yi mian?

你最喜歡什麼樣的意麵？

A I like yi mian served without soup. The braised ground pork sauce on the top is the key. Each vendor has its own sauce.

我最喜歡乾意麵。乾意麵上所淋的肉燥通常是重點。店家都有自己特製的肉燥。

B My favorite is just yi mian mixed with pork lard. It is easy but it is so delicious. My mother used to make us yi mian for a late night snack after we studied hard for tests. She just cooked yi mian and mixed it with homemade lard. It is such a good memory.

我最喜歡意麵拌豬油，很簡單但好吃。媽媽以前在我們晚上很晚唸書肚子餓時，她會簡單的做意麵拌豬油給我們吃。真是美好的回憶。

C I like yi mian with soup. It often comes with a braised egg. I also like to order blanched green vegetables and braised fried tofu.

我喜歡湯意麵，通常裡面會有一顆滷蛋，吃的時候再點一盤燙青菜以及滷油豆腐就是很豐富的一餐。

1 北台灣的文化風情

2 中台灣的魅力風情

3 南台灣的熱力風情

4 東台灣農村風情

Q3 What is the origin of yi mian?
意麵是來自那裡？

A I am not sure. Some say yi mian was invented by people from Fuzhou, who later migrated to Tainan. However, I was told that there is no yi mian in Fuzhou. Fuzhou is a port in southeastern China, capital of Fujian province.

我不確定，有人說意麵是當初福州人遷移到台南時所做的。然而，有人跟我說在福州反而沒聽過福州意麵。福州是中國東南部的港口，是福建省的首都。

B I don't know. I only know that duck egg white is used for making yi mian. I also know that the popular "eel yi mian" uses deep fried yi mian.

我不知道。我只知道做意麵是有用到鴨蛋白，我也知道有名的「鱔魚意麵」就是用炸過的意麵做的。

C It's probably hard to find evidence to prove its origins. I know there are two famous yi mian in Taiwan, one is Nantou yi mian and the other one is Yan Shui yi mian. Yan Shui is in Tainan, my hometown.

我想應該很難證明意麵是來自那裡。我知道在台灣有兩個有名的意麵產地，一個是南投意麵，另一個是鹽水意麵。鹽水在台南，是我的故鄉。

 ## Information 美食報馬仔

　　意麵是南投特產。「源振發南投意麵」位於南投市場裡，已有百年歷史的麵店，南投市場裡的「友德意麵」現已傳承到第二代，創立至今已有近五十年的歷史。三代老店的「萬成意麵」也是在南投市場內。「阿陽意麵老店」是 30 年的古早味有獨特的南投意麵加上古法炒製的新鮮肉燥。「阿章意麵」是老店也是 2007 年意麵王冠軍。

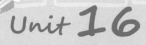

Unit 16
Nantou-Taiwanese old style sandwich
南投－傳統口味營養三明治

 Attractions 景點報報

　　南投竹山有杉林溪、竹海風景區、八通關古道及竹山天梯。竹山文化園區佔地約 6.8 公頃，區內有博物館、產業館以及文化館，到處可以看到竹製品，竹藝術以及竹藤椅，也有竹林隧道的大地竹境步道。竹山的竹林面積有超過一萬公頃，冬筍、桂竹筍、麻竹筍都是這裡的名產。筍乾、筍絲、各式竹筍菜餚都是當地小吃，除了竹子外還有地瓜，以及高品質的杉林溪茶。

 Popular snacks / street food 人氣小吃報報

Taiwanese old style or nutritious sandwich uses a warm and crispy deep fried doughnut-type bread, sliced and filled with tomatoes and cucumbers, ham or sausage, slices of braised hard-boiled egg and Taiwanese sweet mayonnaise. The origins of this sandwich are unknown, and even the mayonnaise may seem out of place from a western point of view. In fact, mayonnaise is the second most popular condiment in nearby Japan – second only to the ubiquitous soy sauce. Mayonnaise was probably introduced to

East Asia from Europe some time during the 19ᵗʰ century. Now, mayonnaise has grown to such a high position in Japan that there is a mayonnaise museum called Mayo Terrace. Mayonnaise is so popular in Taiwan and Japan that American restaurant chains like Pizza Hut put mayonnaise on top of pizza in those countries. While this may sound bizarre to western tastes, globalization of food is not a new thing. Even in the 13ᵗʰ century, Marco Polo, the famous Italian explorer, is part of a legend in which he carries noodles from China back home to Italy. However, Italy strongly protests against the idea that China invented noodles and notes that there is no archeological evidence to support the idea.

 中譯

　　台灣古早味營養三明治是用炸過類似甜甜圈麵團的麵包，切片後加了番茄和黃瓜、火腿或香腸、滷蛋以及台式甜味美奶滋。這種三明治的起源無可考，西方人更想不到會有台式美奶滋這種醬料。事實上，美奶滋在日本是第二個最流行的調味品，僅次於無處不有的醬油。美奶滋可能在 19 世紀由歐洲傳入東亞。現在，美奶滋已經在日本有很崇高的地位，甚至有美乃滋展示館。美乃滋在台灣和日本非常受歡迎，美國的連鎖餐廳像必勝客會把美乃滋加在比薩餅上面。這對西方人來說聽起來匪夷所思，但食物的全球化不是最近才有的。甚至在 13 世紀，有關意大利著名的探險家馬可波羅有一個傳說，他把來自中國的麵條帶回老家義大利。然而，義大利對於中國發明麵條的說法是強烈抗議，表明沒有考古證據。

Q1 Is the fried bread for the sandwich nutritious in some way?

營養三明治的油炸麵包有營養嗎？

A Of course, if a person needs to increase their calorie or fat intake, yes! People needed calories in the olden days for all the hard manual work they did all day long.

當然，對需要增加其熱量和脂肪的攝取量來説，這是有營養的！以前的人們確實需要很多的熱量因為整天都在做繁重的體力勞動。

B No, the dough is made with flour, eggs, sugar, salt, yeast and water. It has the typical ingredients for doughnuts, rolled thick, sliced in oblong shapes and fried. The making process is just like making doughnuts, though the dough has less sugar than doughnuts. Nutrition or not. It is delicious.

不會啊，這種麵團是用高筋麵粉、蛋、細砂糖、鹽、酵母粉和水所做的，這與一般做甜甜圈的材料很類似，麵團擀開做成長的橢

圓形後再炸。製作過程就像做甜甜圈一樣，不過糖加得比較少。不管有沒有營養，很好吃就是。

~~~~~~

C What is your definition of nutritious? I think as a whole, the snack has grains, vegetables, and protein. So, it makes a nutritious and satisfying snack! If you watch the vendor frying the dough, you would want to eat not only one but more.

你所謂的營養的定義是什麼？我認為，整體來說，這個小吃有穀物、蔬菜和蛋白質。因此，應該是營養夠也令人滿意的小吃！如果你看到老闆炸那麵包，你絕對不只想吃一個而已。

Q2 **Are the fresh vegetables safe to eat? I have heard of people getting sick from eating uncooked vegetables in Asia.**
生的蔬菜可以安全食用嗎？我聽說有人在亞洲因為吃未煮過的蔬菜而生病。

Ⓐ Yes, this vendor is very careful to wash the vegetables thoroughly and even soak them in salt water to kill any bacteria that may remain from the farm.

是可以吃的，我知道這個攤販都非常仔細地徹底地清洗蔬菜，甚至把蔬菜稍微浸泡在鹽水中以達到殺菌的效果。

Ⓑ I have also heard of tourists becoming sick from eating fresh vegetables and fruit in other places. There is always a risk to eat any food. I also heard several times about recalled contaminated salad in the US.

我也聽說過遊客因為吃新鮮蔬菜和水果而生病。其實吃任何食物都有風險。我還聽過有幾次美國的沙拉因為受到汙染而大量收回。

C I have advised many visitors to try the sandwich at this vendor's stall. None have become sick from eating here.

我都會跟遊客說去試試這個攤位的營養三明治。沒有人因為在這裡吃過而生病的。

Q3 Do you like mayonnaise?
你喜歡美奶滋嗎？

A When bamboo is in season, my mom buys fresh bamboo from the market. She peels the skin, chops the bamboo into big chunks and cooks it in hot water. After it is cooked, bamboo is cooled and refrigerated. When it is completely cool, mom just tops it with Kewpie mayonnaise.

竹筍季時，我媽媽會去市場買新鮮竹筍，回來就把皮削掉，切大塊後放入水煮熟。竹筍煮熟放入冰箱冰鎮後，上面加美奶滋就很好吃。

B Yes, but only the Japanese style mayonnaise that is on this sandwich. It has sugar and is made with rice vinegar, and it's a bit thinner consistency and sweeter than the thick and more sour mayonnaise you have in the US.

是的。但只在三明治上抹上薄薄的日式美奶滋，這種美奶滋是用米醋做的。這與美國的美奶滋不太一樣。日式美奶滋比較不濃郁也比較甜。美國的美奶滋比較濃郁也比較酸。

C Pizza with mayonnaise is delicious! Here in Taiwan we also put seafood on pizza, the whole shrimp and clam. Corn on pizza is also popular.

比薩上加美奶滋很好吃！在台灣這裡，我們也會把海鮮放在比薩上面，也會放整條蝦和蛤蜊。玉米也是也很受歡迎的比薩食材。

 ## Information 美食報馬仔

「不一樣三明治、甜甜圈」就是不一樣。這個流動攤車位於南投市彰南路上，賣的是台灣古早味的營養三明治、甜甜圈。這裡的三明治就是類似在基隆也很有名的營養三明治，算是台灣早期口味的三明治。位於南投市復興路的小米蛋餅也是隱藏版的在地美食，賣的就只有蛋餅與奶茶，是很受歡迎的下午點心。這兩家是台灣小貨車攤路邊美食的最佳代言。

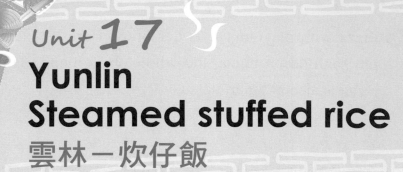

Unit 17
Yunlin
Steamed stuffed rice
雲林－炊仔飯

Attractions 景點報報

斗六市立圖書館是台灣第一座以兒童為主的繪本圖書館，沒有排列整齊的書架、椅子與桌子，取而代之的是夢幻的空間，以激發大人、小孩對閱讀的興趣。找本好書就可以隨意徜徉在非空間限制的閱讀世界裡。這裡就是小朋友幻想中的童話世界，有很炫的天花板、海底世界閱讀區、白雲城堡區、溜滑梯與城堡的組合，室內樓梯旁還有一棵傑克的仙豆樹！小朋友可以爬著仙豆樹樓梯在閱讀中進入另一個想像的國度。

Popular snacks / street food 人氣小吃報報

Tube rice, zhu tong fan, or bamboo rice is a traditional food of indigenous Taiwanese people. This savory dish is made from sticky rice and numerous local ingredients, all cooked but then stuffed into about a 20 cm (8 inch) long mature, green bamboo stalk, then sealed and steamed. Because of the steaming, the rice and ingredients are melded together in a sticky, delicious tower or served in an opened bamboo stalk. The bamboo stalk was an excellent container not only to cook this light meal, but also for early hunters and gatherers to carry some nourishment on their expeditions. Primary ingredients are pork – or wild boar – shitake mushrooms, shallots and shrimp. Street vendors serve it with a delicious sauce and may top it with peanuts, pork thread or cilantro. Steamed stuffed rice is a similar dish using small bowls rather than bamboo stalks. Steamed stuffed rice originated in Yunlin and only can be found in Yunlin. Different from sticky rice used in tube rice, steamed stuffed rice uses regular cooked rice, stuffed with meat sauce and green peas into a small bowl then steamed. Tube rice can be found all over the island but steamed stuffed rice can only be found in Yunlin.

 中譯

　　竹筒飯是台灣原住民的傳統食品。這種美味的菜餚是由糯米和當地食材煮熟後，放入約 20 公分（八吋）的綠竹筒密封好後再蒸熟。因為有蒸過，因此所有的材料會混合在一起，煮好時切開來就可直接食用。竹筒是一種很棒的食材容器，不但能用來煮輕食，早期獵人打獵時也用來盛裝他們的食物。竹筒飯主要成分是野豬肉、香菇、紅蔥和蝦。有些小販會加上美味的醬料和花生、肉鬆或香菜。炊仔飯也是一種類似竹筒飯的美食，是用碗當蒸具而不是竹筒。炊仔飯起源於雲林，也只有在雲林才有。不同於竹筒飯裡所用的糯米，炊仔飯是用一般的米飯，將肉燥、青豆等配料都放到碗裡後再蒸熟。竹筒飯在台灣全島都可以吃的到，但是炊仔飯只有在雲林才有。

Q1 **What are the main ingredients of tube rice?**
竹筒飯裡面通常是有什麼材料呢？

A There can be some variation between different vendors, though the most traditional combination is minced pork, shallots, shitake mushrooms, and shrimp with the rice. Some vendors may add the flavors of egg, peanut and cilantro to satisfy different tastes.

不同賣家會做不同材料的變化，但最傳統的材料是豬肉、紅蔥頭、香菇、蝦與糯米。有一些賣家可能會加雞蛋、花生、香菜口味以滿足不同的口味。

B Originally, the indigenous people used what they could find or kill in the wild: Rice, wild onions, wild mushrooms, and wild boar.

起初原住民是用他們能找到材料或野外可以抓到的動物：大米、野蔥、野蘑菇和野豬。

C Sticky rice is the most important ingredient, but the flavor comes from the pork, shallots, mushrooms, and – in the coastal areas – shrimp.

糯米是最重要的材料，但好味道是來自於豬肉、蔥、香菇還有沿海地區的蝦。

How is tube rice different from steamed stuffed rice?

竹筒飯與炊仔飯有什麼不一樣呢？

A Tube rice is cooked in a bamboo tube. For the indigenous people, bamboo – which grows so quickly – was plentiful and sustainable. The moisture from the bamboo would really do the steaming when the dish was baked over hot coals. The bamboo adds a fresh, bright taste to the richness of the meat, onions, and mushrooms.

竹筒飯是飯在竹筒裡煮熟的。對於原住民來說，竹子長得快，豐富也能持續取得的。竹子中的水份，在炭火上烘烤時有加速蒸熟的效果。竹子也在肉、蔥、和蘑菇的濃烈味道中，增添了清新的口感。

B The most famous local food in Douliu, Yunlin is steamed stuffed rice. All ingredients are pre-cooked. Add cooked peas, meat sauce and shredded eggs to the bottom of a stainless bowl then add rice. Steam several small bowls it in a large cypress bowl for 15 minutes. Before serving, add braised meat sauce on top. The cypress smell gives this dish a unique aroma.

雲林斗六最有名的地方小吃就是炊仔飯。所有的食材都要先煮過，把碗豆、肉燥跟蛋絲舖在碗底，再熟米飯，將數個小碗放到檜木桶裡蒸 15 分鐘，要吃時再淋上滷肉汁，炊仔飯的檜木香氣很獨特。

C I am from Tainan. I have never heard of steamed stuffed rice. I just googled it and it is not a Tainan dish. It is only in Yunlin.

我是台南人。我從來沒有聽說過這種炊仔飯。我用谷歌搜索資料，這不是台南菜。只有在雲林才有。

Q3 Most people know about tube rice but not steamed stuffed rice. Do you know about it?

很多人聽過竹筒飯，但是沒有聽過炊仔飯，你對炊仔飯知道有多少？

A Add braised chopped pork, peas and shredded eggs to a stainless bowl. Add cooked rice. Steam the bowl in a steamer. The best sauce for this is lard with soy sauce.

炊仔飯是把肉燥、豌豆、蛋絲等配料先鋪放到不鏽鋼的碗裡，再把米飯覆蓋在上面，連碗帶飯，用大蒸籠保溫。豬油加醬油是最搭的醬汁。

B Every vendor has slightly different ingredients. The one I like has egg, meat sauce, peas, and sliced meat balls. I also liked to order a dish of blanched water spinach which is topped with meat sauce, soy sauce and mashed garlic.

每一家的味道都有一點不一樣。我喜歡的炊仔飯是有蛋絲、肉燥、青豆仁和貢丸，我吃的時候也會點燙空心菜，空心菜會淋上肉燥、醬油膏和蒜泥。

C When you eat steamed stuffed rice, you must have steamed eggs and another bowl of pig blood soup. That's a perfect meal. Day lily soup is also a good choice.

炊仔飯一定要搭配蒸蛋，加上一碗豬血湯，那才是完美的一餐。金針湯也是不錯的選擇。

 ## *Information* 美食報馬仔

　　炊仔飯是斗六的特有小吃。壹品炊仔飯、斗六炊仔飯與蕃薯仔炊仔飯都是當地很有名氣的老店。很多學生會推薦木火炊仔飯因為經濟實惠，物美價廉。炊仔飯價格都很親民，一碗炊仔飯，搭配肉羹或蒸蛋就是可以吃飽飽的一餐。炊仔飯的特點很像家常白飯，吃過的人都說炊仔飯的特點在於米飯粒粒分明，醬汁清爽不油膩，這是雲林才有的古早味。

Unit 18
Yunlin-pan fried steamed rice cake (Jian Pan Guo)
雲林－煎盤粿

Attractions 景點報報

雲林北港歷史街區是北港老街最熱鬧的地方。從街道指標可以到義民廟、蔡培火故居、朝天宮與百年古井。北港義民廟是紀念台灣早期閩籍義民抗清朝的民變事件。蔡培火是日治時期重要的政治及社會運動人士。這裡也有舊時代的振興戲院，經過整修保留了戲院挑高的原有空間，這是台灣最完整的老戲院。老街的另一頭是北港觀光大橋，北港最有名的就是「麻油」，在這裡到處都聞得到很香的麻油香味。

Popular snacks / street food 人氣小吃報報

Street vendors throughout Taiwan can be found selling the traditional turnip cake or lo bak go, even during breakfast hours. The name is a bit misleading though, because Chinese radish or the Japanese daikon is the root vegetable that makes up the largest ingredient in this treat, not turnip. Since it is among the Cantonese dim sum offerings, we can assume that lo bak go traveled with the Hakka people to Taiwan from southern China at some point. The cake is a savory dish, and not a spongy, sweet cake like some westerners may envision "cake" to be. Steaming is a common cooking method in many Taiwanese dishes and the result is called a cake, especially if the preparation includes blending many ingredients into a homogenous mass prior to steaming. While grated radish and rice flour make up the base, scallion, mushroom, and sausage may be mixed in before the cake is steamed. After nearly an hour of steaming, the cake is typically sliced and pan fried for additional flavor and the crispy outside edges. In Yulin, the locals have their own version of Chinese radish cake or pan fried steamed rice cake (Jian Pan Guo). It does not have Chinese radish.

 中譯

　　在台灣有很多攤販會賣傳統的蘿蔔糕，即使在早餐時間也是很普遍的。這個名字是有點誤導的，因為所謂的蘿蔔或日本蘿蔔是根性植物，是很普遍的食材，但是通常蘿蔔在英文被翻譯為 turnip，其實是蕪菁。蘿蔔糕是港式點心，所以我們可以臆斷是從中國南方來的客家人當時把蘿蔔糕帶入台灣。蘿蔔糕是很美味的，但是糕跟西方人所熟悉的甜點、糕點是南轅北轍。「蒸」在台灣菜餚的烹飪是很常見的方法，特別是如果製造過程是需要許多材料混合成泥狀都會用到「蒸」的方式，蒸出來的成品就叫「糕」。蘿蔔刨成絲狀後還會加上再來米，紅蔥頭，香菇，香腸。材料混合後經過近蒸一小時，放涼切片煎的脆脆的就是蘿蔔糕。在雲林，有類似蘿蔔糕當地自己的特殊版本叫煎盤粿，這是沒有加蘿蔔只有純米做成的糕。

Q1 Luo bo gao and pan fried steamed rice cake seem very similar. Are they difficult to make?

蘿蔔糕與煎盤粿很類似，這種美食很難做嗎？

A It's not difficult to make Luo bo gao, though there are many steps involved. You must first grate the radish and chop sausage, mushroom, and scallion. Then you add rice flour and combine all the ingredients prior to spreading it in the pan for steaming.

蘿蔔糕不難做，但是需要有幾個步驟。首先要先刨蘿蔔，把香腸、香菇、紅蔥頭都切碎。加入在來米粉以及所有的成分混合後，在鍋子裡蒸熟。

B I never heard of pan fried steamed rice cake but I make Luo bo gao at home. If you have a grater for the radish and a large steamer, it is not difficult.

我從來沒有聽過煎盤粿，但我自己在家裡做蘿蔔糕。如果你有一個刨器可以刨蘿蔔和一個大蒸籠，這樣做起來就並不難。

C Pan fried steamed rice cake ingredients are glutinous rice flour, water, salt, sugar, wheat starch, chestnut flour, pepper and oil. Wash and soak the rice and grind it. Mix it with the rest of the ingredients and steam it. That is steamed rice cake.

煎盤粿的基本材料是在來米粉，水、鹽、糖、澄粉、馬蹄粉、胡椒粉與沙拉油。米洗淨、浸泡、瀝乾後磨漿，再加入其餘材料拌勻。蒸熟後就是煎盤粿。

1 北台灣的文化風情

2 中台灣的魅力風情

3 南台灣的熱力風情

4 東台灣農村風情

Q2 Do people eat pan fried steamed rice cake for breakfast?

真的有人把煎盤粿當早餐嗎？

A Taiwan is very small but eating habits are quite different between regions. My friend from Yulin said that their breakfasts are pan fried steamed rice cake, thread noodle soup, peanut oily rice and fish soup. Breakfast for many people in the south is fried noodles, beef soup, braised meat rice and thick noodle soup.

台灣這麼小但是南北的飲食文化差異很大。雲林北港的朋友說他們的早餐是吃煎盤粿、麵線糊、土豆油飯、草魚湯。很多人在南部的早餐是炒麵、牛肉湯，滷肉飯和肉羹麵。

B Yes. We grow up eating pan fried steamed rice cake. Many people in Taiwan never heard of it. The fried steamed rice cake is topped with sweet rice sauce. It is a little sweet and very delicious.

是啊。我們小時候就是吃煎盤粿長大的。很多人在台灣沒有聽過這個。煎盤粿會加入甜的糯米醬，吃起來甜甜的，很美味。

C That's right, but only in Yulin. The rice cake is made with glutinous rice flour. It goes really well with the braised big intestine. Yes, big intestine for breakfast.

沒錯。這是只有在雲林才有的早餐。在來米製成的粿，配上滷大腸很搭。是的，早餐吃大腸頭。

Q3 What's in rice sausage that usually comes with pan fried steamed rice cake?
煎盤粿都會點的米腸是怎麼做的呢？

A Rice sausage is made with polished glutinous rice mixed with shallots, soy sauce, five spice powder and peanut. Put the mixture in casings (cleaned intestines) to make the sausage. Add ginger in the water to cook with the rice sausage.

糯米腸是將糯米、油蔥油、醬油、五香粉和花生攪拌後灌入處理好的豬腸中，滾水入薑片一起煮。

B Rice sausage is commonly made with rice and peanuts. However, in the south, my mother used to make the rice sausage with lima beans instead of peanuts. Now it is hard to find rice sausage with lima beans.

糯米腸通常是有米和花生。但是，在南部，我媽媽以前會加青豆，不是加花生。現在很少看到有加青豆的米腸。

C Rice sausage is made with the smaller intestines of a pig, special spices, red shallots, peanuts, and lard, and glutinous rice. Pan fried steamed rice cake goes so good with rice sausage. I also like to have a bowl of pig blood soup too.

糯米腸是用豬腸衣、特製香料、新鮮紅蔥頭、油蔥酥、花生、豬油及糯米所做的。煎盤粿配上米腸真的很搭。我還喜歡配上一碗豬血湯。

 ### *Information* 美食報馬仔

　　煎盤粿是除了雲林以外很多台灣人沒有聽過的早餐。北港煎盤粿、金捷發煎盤粿、陳家煎盤粿、阿婆煎盤粿、小叮噹煎盤粿、巧妙煎盤粿都是北港人最常吃的早餐。煎盤粿很像蘿蔔糕但其實就是米粿，因為製作過程中沒有蘿蔔，只有用米粉蒸成。綜合煎盤粿就是米粿外層煎到外層香脆加上北港香腸、滷大腸和米腸，再加上米漿和醬油調製的沾醬與一碗清湯，這就是真正的北港鄉土古早味。

1 北台灣的文化風情

2 中台灣的魅力風情

3 南台灣的熱力風情

4 東台灣農村風情

Unit 19
Chiayi turkey rice
嘉義－火雞肉飯

Attractions 景點報報

　　嘉義縣竹崎鄉竹崎公園入口就有一台早期的阿里山森林鐵路的小火車。千禧吊橋、八二三砲戰紀念園區，還有台灣最長吊橋的弘景吊橋。天空走廊約 185 公尺，行走上頭可以看見公園的不同樣貌。大人小孩都喜歡的親水區也是看山色的好地方，花仙子步道盤騰在樹林間，全長約 400 公尺，夏天走在這裡是涼爽舒適。整個園區走完可能要規劃 3 小時以上。這樣的公園是不用門票的。

Popular snacks / street food 人氣小吃報報

Turkey rice is a light, rustic dish that contrasts well with the rich, fried, complex offerings at many Taiwanese night markets. The turkey is typically steamed, as many traditional Taiwanese dishes are, then shredded and prepared simply with fried shallots, salt, pepper, a tiny bit of soy sauce, sugar, and Sichuan pepper. A big scoop of rice in a bowl, topped with the turkey and sauce is the common way to enjoy this aromatic and tasty meal. Chiayi City has a great tradition with turkey rice, and also a great tradition of

fostering open dialogue about a taboo topic in Taiwanese society:
the 228 Incident. The entire topic was taboo for decades. Chiayi's
city government was the first in Taiwan to establish a monument
to remember the Incident.

　　跟許多台灣夜市很多豐富或炸過的小吃比較來説，火雞肉飯是
一道很簡單道地的菜。這種火雞要蒸過，就像許多傳統的台灣菜是用
蒸的一樣，然後切絲，醬汁是用炒過的紅蔥頭，鹽，胡椒粉，醬油，
糖和花椒做成的，盛一碗飯，擺上火雞肉，淋上醬汁，就是一道平常
品嘗香馥美味火雞肉飯吃法。嘉義市的火雞飯很有名，嘉義也是當年
二二八事件的話題。這個禁忌話題被禁了好幾十年。嘉義市政府後來
建立台灣第一個二二八紀念碑。

Q1 **How is the turkey prepared? Is it roasted in the oven like we do in the US?**
火雞是怎麼煮的？是像在美國那樣在烤箱內烤的嗎？

A Believe it or not, the turkey is steamed in a large pot.

你可能不相信，這種火雞肉是在大鍋子裡蒸熟的。

B It's very moist, isn't it? That's because the cook actually steams the turkey in a large pot – just like you might steam vegetables. The best turkey size for this dish is about 16.8 kg.

火雞肉肉汁多，對嗎？那是因為火雞是在一個大鍋裡蒸熟 – 就像蒸蔬菜一樣。火雞一定要選 16.8 公斤以上的大小。

C First the cook steams the turkey in a pot, then sautés shallots in lard, adding reserved juices from the turkey plus the spices, sugar, and soy sauce. This sauce is poured over the steamed turkey just at the point of serving the dish. Also, the rice for turkey rice has to be local Hsi Luo rice from Taiwan. Perfectly cooked rice will soak up the sauce for the best result.

首先要先在一個大鍋裡蒸煮熟火雞,然後用豬油爆香紅蔥頭,加入預留的、用香料、糖、醬油所醃過火雞肉煮過的醬汁。要吃的時候在飯上淋上醬汁。此外,還需要蒸的完美的米粒才能好吸收醬汁。

What side dishes are usually eaten with turkey rice?

火雞肉飯通常會有什麼樣的配菜？

A Napa with dried fish, braised bean curd and miso soup are the common side dishes that are served with turkey rice in my hometown.

扁魚白菜、油豆腐和味增湯是我家鄉那裡吃火雞肉飯常見的配菜。

B I prefer chicken rice. The style is very similar. The best part of chicken rice is the pickled radish and sour greens. Vendors usually offer different types of soup. I love gizzard soup, pineapple soup, chicken feet soup and fish ball soup.

我比較喜歡吃雞肉飯，這兩種其實很類似。吃雞肉飯最配的是醃蘿蔔和酸菜。通常都會有不同湯可選擇。下水湯、鳳梨苦瓜、雞爪湯和魚丸湯都是我的最愛。

C One time we visited the south for a holiday trip, we ate turkey rice. We ordered two bowls of rice, blanched edible ferns and bitter gourd and rib soup. For us from Taipei, these types of food are very satisfying and inexpensive. We were full and the price for that lunch was about the same as a cup of coffee from Starbucks.

有一次我們去南部度假時吃了火雞肉飯。我們點了兩碗飯、過貓和苦瓜排骨湯。就以台北物價來說，這種小吃真的很實在，也不貴。當時吃了一桌我們覺得吃得很飽，卻也才不過是北部一杯星巴克咖啡的價格。

Q3 Is the turkey a native bird of Taiwan?
火雞是台灣的原生鳥類嗎？

A No the turkey is not native to Taiwan. I believe it was imported when the Dutch colonists ruled Taiwan centuries ago.

不是的，火雞不是原產於台灣。我想這是荷蘭在幾個世紀前殖民統治台灣時所帶進來的。

B No, it is not, though there are many other game birds from Taiwan, including varieties of pheasants, quails, ducks, and geese.

不，不是的，火雞不是台灣原產的。但是很多其他的可食性的鳥類，品種包括野雞，鵪鶉，鴨和鵝是原產於台灣。

C I don't think so. There are small turkey farms though, especially in this central and southern region of the country.

我不這麼認為。但是現在在台灣有小型的火雞養殖場，尤其是在中部和南部地區。

 ## Information 美食報馬仔

屬於嘉義人的笑話有此一說，嘉義人對好吃的火雞肉飯都有不同看法，但是對不好吃的火雞肉飯都有相同的看法。劉里長雞肉飯有 30 幾年歷史，是三代經營的，劉里長還真的是里長伯。郭家雞肉飯在文化夜市裡；郭家除雞肉飯與粿仔湯是招牌小吃。「嘉義噴水雞肉飯」是全台有名也是觀光客必到之處。民主火雞肉飯曾在火雞肉飯節被評選為優選獎，乾淨的用餐環境也是饕客喜愛的特色之一。

Unit 20
Chiayi Tofu pudding, doufu hua, douhua
嘉義－豆花

 Attractions 景點報報

　　嘉義市內的嘉油鐵馬道（Jiayou Bicycle Trail）是廢棄鐵路所改修的自行車專用車道，鐵道路幅很寬敞，全長 4.75 公里，二側是單車道與人行道，這是城市居民輕鬆散步運動的路線，整個路線共經過了 3 個里和 3 個村，沿途有小型的親水公園，也有很多休憩點，可以休閒、散步、更是騎自行車的好地方。唯一美中不足的是有些路段是進入嘉義市會遇到平面道路交叉路口，要通過時須留意左右來車，騎到底就是北回歸線。

 Popular snacks / street food 人氣小吃報報

Tofu pudding, doufu hua, douhua, or translated directly "tofu flower" is a simple, traditional dessert, forms of which you can find around East Asia. The Taiwan form can be cold in summer or warm in winter, but always refreshing. Rolling carts of soy milk vendors were common in earlier days, bringing their product into neighborhoods and making all the kids beg their mothers for a little money to buy this treat. It is simply soy milk made fresh daily into a gelatin-like form, floating in a thin brown sugar syrup and topped with sweetened black beans, red beans, or peanuts. In other parts of Asia, there might be ginger or almond in the syrup, or it may also be savory and served for breakfast. It is possible to find these forms of tofu pudding also in Taiwan, but the most traditional is simply topped with sugar syrup. Chiayi county has a strong, diverse economy with lumber from the Ali mountains in the west, central location for strong transportation and communication sectors, plus strong industry and educational institutions. Chiayi hosts a famous international music festival during the last two weeks of December, providing performance and learning opportunities for participants from across the globe.

 ## 中譯

　　豆腐布丁、豆腐花、豆花，或直接翻譯成「豆花」其實就是一個簡單的、傳統的甜點，這在東南亞很普遍。台灣的豆花在夏天是吃冷的，在冬天是吃溫的，兩種吃法都會讓人很驚喜。在早期流動豆漿攤販是很常見的，他們在社區裡賣豆花，很多孩子就會向媽媽討一點錢來買這種甜點。這其實是豆漿做成有膠狀的甜點，在上面淋上黑糖漿加上甜黑豆、紅豆或花生。在亞洲其他地區，有些地方會加薑或杏仁的糖漿，或是做成鹹的，或者也有人當早餐吃。在台灣這種口味的豆花也很普遍，但真正傳統的口味只是淋上糖漿。嘉義縣因為有阿里山山脈生產木材而有強大也多樣化的經濟與運輸和通信行業，也有很不錯的產業和教育機構。嘉義在 12 月的最後兩個星期會舉辦來自世界各地的國際著名音樂節，提供參加者表演和學習的機會。

Q1 **How does the cook turn the soy milk into this solid form?**
豆漿是要怎麼做才會變成固態的形式？

Ⓐ A coagulant solidifies the protein and oil in hot soy milk. There are many different types of coagulants that do this, with varying effects. The most popular types of additives are gypsum (calcium sulphate) and Japanese nigari. Nigari is a common additive used for making soft tofu.

有一種凝固劑會讓熱豆漿裡的蛋白質和油凝固。市面上有許多種類的凝結劑會有這種效果。最普遍的添加劑是石膏（硫酸鈣）和日本海鹽濃縮液。軟豆腐通常會用海鹽濃縮液來做。

Ⓑ In Japan, the cook might use gelatin to do so, but here in Taiwan it is most authentic to use gypsum. The gypsum adds a little sweetness as well.

在日本是使用明膠，但在台灣最原始的是使用石膏。石膏會增添一些甜味。

C Actually, I don't know. Gypsum, maybe?

我其實不知道。有可能是石膏。

Q2 Are there any toppings on a bowl of tofu pudding?
豆花上面有什麼加料呢？

A There are too many topping options to name, but really just the silky soy pudding and syrup are satisfying by themselves. The toppings are a bonus! Longan topping was my grandfather's favorite. It is a good memory of my childhood.

其實有很多不同的加料，說不完的。但實際上豆花加糖漿就可以令人很滿足了。若有加料也不錯啦！桂圓豆花是我阿公的最愛，這也就成了我的童年記憶。

B What do you like? There are a lot of choices for toppings: tapioca, taro balls, yam balls, lotus seeds, cooked oatmeal, beans, peanuts and fruits. I love lotus seeds. I also like peanut topping. It usually has a little almond taste.

你喜歡什麼樣的加料呢？有很多的選擇：粉圓、芋頭、番薯、蓮子、薏仁、甜豆、花生和水果都有。我很喜歡 蓮子豆花，我也喜歡花生豆花，這種口味有一點杏仁味道。

C Many toppings contain that great chewy texture the Taiwanese love. For example, there are tapioca, various steamed balls like those made of taro or sweet potato, and of course sweetened black, red, or mung beans.

許多配料都是台灣人喜愛的 Q 勁。例如，有小粉圓，或芋頭或甘藷粉做的不同粉圓，當然也有甜的黑豆、紅豆或綠豆。

1 北台灣的文化風情

2 中台灣的魅力風情

3 南台灣的熱力風情

4 東台灣農村風情

Q3 Where we live in the west, we normally think of pudding as cold. Is tofu pudding a cold dessert?

在西方，我們通常認為布丁是一種冷的甜點。豆花是冷的甜點嗎？

A It is cold – even served with ice – in the warmer months of the year, but in the cooler months, tofu pudding is served warm.

在比較熱的季節是吃冷的，有時豆花還會加冰一起吃呢，但在較冷的季節，豆花是吃溫的。

B It's refreshing to have the cold tofu pudding during Taiwan's long hot and humid season, but warm tofu pudding is so comforting to the digestive system when the air is a bit chilly. It is doubly good for the digestion if you happen to find the type of pudding with a little ginger in the sauce. It really calms your stomach after you eat all that greasy street food!

在台灣這種長期高溫高濕度的天氣，豆花吃起來是很清爽的，但是當天氣比較涼的時候，溫溫的豆花其實吃起來對消化系統是很

好的。如果你有吃過薑汁豆花，這對消化系統更很有用。尤其吃過所有油膩的街頭小吃後，這種甜點真的會鎮定你的胃！

C It's mainly a cold dessert, and just sweet enough to finish off a long evening trying all of Taiwan's delicious street food.

這主要是一種甜點，這種甜點的甜度很適合吃完台灣的夜市美食後品嘗。

 ## Information 美食報馬仔

　　台灣一般的豆花都是糖水豆花，但是嘉義豆花的吃法是加豆漿不是加糖水，內行人說這種吃法可以保存豆花的香味與品質。「阿娥豆花」是嘉義市文化夜市裡的必吃小吃。阿娥豆花便宜又好吃，是大排長龍的必吃甜點。豆漿豆花、粉圓豆花、綜合豆花都是很多人的最愛。嘉義市東區的皇家豆花也是優質豆花專賣店，很有 Q 勁的「珍珠豆花」值得一嘗。

Part 3

南台灣的熱力風情

Unit 21
Tainan
Gwa Bow
台南－割包

Attractions 景點報報

　　台南這個城市因為幾百年來不同外人遷入而逐漸形成有歷史意義的古城，福建人、廣東人，荷蘭人、日本人在台南慢慢建立飲食風格。位於臺南市國華街三段的永樂市場就可以吃到台南小吃的代表：蚵仔粥或虱目魚粥、春捲、肉粽、米糕、碗粿、擔仔麵和青草茶。永樂市場有名的金三角就是金得春捲、富盛號碗粿以及阿松豬舌割包。台南美食的最高境界就是一直吃一直吃，台南美食會讓遊客吃到離開後還是戀戀不忘。

Popular snacks / street food 人氣小吃報報

Gwa Bow (刈包) is bun with braised pork belly. Gwa Bow literally means slice the bun in Taiwanese. Instead of Gwa Bow, other places in Taiwan name it "Tiger biting pig" (hoo-ka-ti) simply because it looks like something in a tiger's mouth. It is originally from Fuzhou, China. It is also called Taiwanese Hamburger. It has become a popular street food in Taiwan. The popular Gwa Bow has five basic components: the white fluffy steamed bun, tender braised pork belly, pickled mustard greens, fresh cilantro, and powdered peanuts. The most famous Gwa Bow in Tainan is A-Song Gwa Bow (阿松割包) located in Yong Le market (永樂市場) in Tainan. The second generation owner's father learned the traditional way of making Gwa Bow in Fuzhou, China. According to the owner, the real traditional Gwa Bow has pig tongue and pork belly that are cooked for hours until tender. Then it is cooked again with red rice yeast, Chinese angelica and many other Chinese medicine ingredients for another hour. The ready-to-use pig tongue and pork belly are a little pinkish because of red rice yeast.

 中譯

　　「刈包」就是饅頭裡加滷五花肉。割包在台灣話裡直接翻譯就是把蒸包切開。台灣其他地方把刈包稱為虎咬豬，因為從外表看起來很像老虎的大嘴咬了一塊豬肉。刈包源自中國福州，也稱作台灣漢堡。這是很受歡迎的台灣小吃。割包通常有五種基本材料：特製白饅頭、紅燒五花肉、醃菜、香菜和花生粉。台南最有名的刈包是阿松割包，位於台南永樂市場。第二代店主的父親早年在福州學到傳統割包的做法，根據老闆的說法，傳統的刈包是有瘦肉、豬舌等，這些材料是煮到爛熟後再加入紅糖、當歸以及很多中藥材，再滷一個小時，刈包裡的肉是淺紅色的因為有加紅糖或紅麴。

Q & A 外國人都是這樣問 ((◎)) *MP3 21*

Q1 **Do you bake the bun that is used for Gwa Bow?**
你會將割包用的圓饅頭烘培嗎?

A No. It is actually a steamed bun.

沒有,那其實是用蒸的。

B Probably not. A yeast bun, although not an ingredient itself, is served as a base or cover for several ingredients. It influences how customers feel about the whole dish. Often western bread involves a baking process. Through baking, the bun has a different taste, and the flavor varies, too. Customers can have a distaste for the food if the bun is not right. I often see it is steamed in a bamboo steamer.

應該不會。圓麵包,儘管本身不是成分的一種,是充當食物基底或包覆幾種原料的外層。它影響著顧客對整個菜餚的觀感。通常西式麵包牽涉烘培的過程。透過烘培,圓麵包有著不同的味道,

而這些風味也跟著有所不同。若圓麵包的感覺不對，顧客可能對食物感到厭惡。我常常看到的是放在竹蒸籠裡蒸的。

C No, the bun is not baked. It is similar to a white steamed bun. It is different from western bread. Baking was really not part of traditional Taiwanese food. In old times, people steamed a lot with their wood burning stove, creating such treats as steamed bun, steamed sweets and steamed rice.

沒有。這種圓饅頭不是用烤的，是與白饅頭相似的。跟西式的麵包完全不一樣。在傳統的臺灣食物中不會用到烘焙的部分。在以前，人們會用要燒柴火的灶去蒸包子、甜食及米飯。

Q2 Have you ever tried Gwa Bow with pig tongue?
那你有吃豬舌割包嗎？

A No. I didn't dare. It sounded just too weird. I just cannot eat it. I just had the one with pork belly. It was very good.

沒有耶。我不太敢試。聽起來太怪異了。我真的不敢吃。我只有吃五花肉的。真的很讚喔！

B Yes. I love it. Pig tongue has a very unique taste. It is almost crunchy when you first bite it. It goes really well with the pickled white radish. The peanut sauce is perfect too. Every bite of it is amazing. It was a very thick peanut sauce. I love it so much that I even ordered a pig tongue soup. It is just amazingly different.

有，我超喜歡的。豬舌真的很特別。第一口咬下去幾乎是脆的，跟酸菜還有醃過的白蘿蔔片十分清爽好吃！花生醬更是一絕。咬

下去的每一口都很棒。搭配的花生醬口感非常濃郁。我超喜歡豬舌包的，我甚至還點了一碗豬舌湯。真的是太特別的美味了！

C No. I don't want to kiss the pig tongue. I feel the pig will come after me in the middle of the night and try to kiss me. No, thank you!

沒，我才不想親豬的舌頭呢。我覺得那隻豬會在半夜追著我要跟我接吻。謝了，我才不要。

Q3 **For Taiwanese hamburger, what's the sour greens topping made of?**
中式漢堡裡面的那個酸菜配料是什麼做的？

A It is made with Jay-tsai, a type of mustard plant. My grandmother used to make it. It is just Jay-tsai soaked in salt water and fermented for sourness. She used to make it every year and when it was ready, she always put it in the refrigerator. It is a great accompaniment.

是用芥菜做的，是一種芥菜類的蔬菜。我的阿媽以前常會製作起來備用。是將芥菜浸泡在鹽水中，讓它發酵生出酸味。她以前每年都會做，她會將醃好的酸菜放在冰箱。是個很棒的下飯菜。

B Lots of Taiwanese dishes are served with sour greens. I don't know how to make it. I know it is cheap and you can buy it easily.

有很多的臺灣菜都會配上酸菜喔。我不知道怎麼製作酸菜。我知道它很便宜，而且很容易就能買得到。

C I don't know but it's a great condiment for travelers because it doesn't spoil easily. I had it in a lunch box I bought on the train to Kaoshiung. I also had it in a beef noodle soup.

我不知道，不過對旅行者而言，酸菜是很棒的佐料，因為它不易壞。我在去高雄的火車上所買到的便當裡就有那個。我在吃牛肉麵的時候也有配酸菜。

 ## *Information* 美食報馬仔

　　淺草青春新天地是舊有南市西門公有零售市場，西門市場是日據時代所建的台南市第一個公有市場，周邊有許多特色小攤，也可以走走晃晃二手市集。市場裡知名的江水號的八寶冰店、老店的餛飩湯和意麵也都是逛台南不可錯過的景點！虎尾寮公有零售市場、東菜市公有零售市場和金華公有零售市場，也都是可以吃盡台南美食的好地方。

Unit 22
Tainan
Shrimp fried rice
台南－蝦米飯

Attractions 景點報報

　　赤崁樓是荷蘭人在西元 1653 年所建。幾百年來的赤崁樓因不同政權的轉換而被用來做不同用途，如火藥軍械的貯存所、日語學校臺南分校、台南歷史館，現在則是國家的一級古蹟。赤崁樓旁邊的市集古稱石精臼。這裡有很多老字號的小吃店。赤崁樓附近有祀典武廟，這個古廟保存十分完整，有 300 年以上的歷史。「大天后宮」則是台灣第一座媽祖廟，這兩座廟都位在永福路上。

Popular snacks / street food 人氣小吃報報

Some say that Tainan is the cultural and export center of the island. The city specializes in preserving Taiwanese culture, but was also once host to Fort Zeelandia – the Dutch port that was the primary city from which that country traded with E. Asia. Beginning in the early 1600s, the Dutch East India Company at what is now Tainan was trying to get a piece of the successful spice trade that Spain operated from Manila and the Portugese operated on Macau. The Dutch also recognized the fertile soils in the area and established European style agricultural ventures, growing and exporting wheat, ginger, and tobacco. From Tainan, the Dutch not only brought much spice and porcelain back to the west, but also untold riches to the profit of their European investors. Today, Tainan is the second largest city of Taiwan. Inexpensive stir fry restaurants are found everywhere. A typical family meal – whether eaten at home or while dining out – might consist of three or four such dishes to share, plus soup. It's the classic Taiwanese alternative to the British fish and chips or the American burger and fries. Inexpensive, quickly prepared, and broadly enjoyed.

 中譯

　　有人說，台南是這個島上的文化和出口中心。這個城市保有很棒的閩南文化，這裡也有安平古堡，這個港口是當時荷蘭定為主要可以與亞洲各國交易的城市。始於 17 世紀初，荷蘭東印度公司當時為了成功與占領馬尼拉的西班牙，據有澳門的葡萄牙爭奪香料貿易，而在現在的台南據點。荷蘭人知道台南地區有肥沃的土壤，建立了歐洲風格的農業企業，種植和出口小麥、生薑和煙草。荷蘭人從台南不僅把很多的香料和瓷器運回西方，同時讓他們的歐洲投資者得到很高的利潤。在台南簡單的小吃到處都有。便宜的快炒店隨處可見。一般家庭無論是在家裡吃或外出用餐，大概會有三道或四道菜一起分享，再加上一碗湯。這種典型的台灣菜就好像是英國的炸魚排和薯條或是美國的漢堡薯條。

Q & A 外國人都是這樣問 🔊)) *MP3 22*

Q1 What types of vegetables are commonly included in the stir fry?
熱炒店通常會用什麼樣的蔬菜？

Ⓐ There are so many kinds of vegetables that can be included, though my favorite combination is stir fry cabbage. Taiwan's cabbage tastes so much better than the western cabbage. Taiwan's cabbage is juicy and crunchy.

有很多種蔬菜，但是我最喜歡的是快炒高麗菜。台灣的高麗菜比起西方的高麗菜好吃多了，台灣的高麗菜多汁又鮮脆。

Ⓑ Mushrooms, carrots, celery, napa cabbage, bamboo shoots, green onion – you name it. But never broccoli! Broccoli is only a recent import vegetable in Taiwan.

香菇、胡蘿蔔、芹菜、白菜、冬筍、蔥，只要你説的出來，我們都有。我從來沒有看過快炒店會用綠色花椰菜！綠色花椰菜在台灣是屬於比較最近的進口菜。

C The vegetables can be whatever was on sale at the market, or whatever is in season. It is usually quick, easy and filling. For example, when I go to a stir fry restaurant, I usually order a bowl of rice, a vegetable stir fry, some meat or sausage and a bowl of soup. That's good enough for a full meal.

快炒店的蔬菜通常是超市在特價,或是當季的菜。通常是炒起來很快、容易做、又可以吃得飽的菜。比如,我去快炒店通常會點一碗飯、一盤青菜,一盤香腸,還有一碗湯就夠飽餐一頓。

1 北台灣的文化風情

2 中台灣的魅力風情

3 南台灣的熱力風情

4 東台灣農村風情

Q2 What's your favorite stir fry dish?
你最喜歡的快炒是什麼？

A I had a shrimp fried rice and Giant grouper soup in Tainan. It was rice fried with shrimp, garlic and scrambled eggs. It was really delicious.

我在台南吃過蝦米飯和石斑魚湯。蝦米飯是有蝦米、蒜頭、炒蛋，真是好吃。

B I love stir fried spinach. Other stir fry vegetables are good too. When it is freshly made, it is always good. I had oyster egg. The oyster was in season and it was juicy and inexpensive. The oyster egg dipped in ketchup was a perfect taste.

我很喜歡炒波菜。其他炒青菜也都不錯。當場現炒的都很好吃。我也有吃過蚵仔蛋，蚵仔正當季時，新鮮肥美也不貴，蚵仔和蛋共煎沾蕃茄醬很對味。

C I had a stir fried sweet and sour fish colloid in Tainan. The taste was unforgettable. Fish colloid does not have much taste so black vinegar and onion was added to the dish. I like all kinds of stir fried fish, such as fish stomach, fish meat, fish head and even fish intestine.

我在台南吃過炒酸辣魚膠，那真是吃過忘不了的味道。魚膠無味，配上酸烏醋和甜洋蔥很對味。我喜歡各式熱炒魚肉，炒魚肚、魚肉、魚頭和魚內臟都喜歡。

1 北台灣的文化風情

2 中台灣的魅力風情

3 南台灣的熱力風情

4 東台灣農村風情

Q3 What kinds of menu items does a stir fry restaurant usually have?
快炒店通常會用什麼樣的菜單呢？

A It depends on where you are in Taiwan. In Tainan, because it is a coastal city, seafood stir fry is really popular.

這要看你是在台灣的哪裡。就台南來說，因為它是一個沿海城市，海鮮類快炒是非常受歡迎的。

B It usually offers rice, soup, meat dish, vegetable dish. Some stir fry restaurants even offer hot pot.

通常提供米飯、湯、肉類與菜類。有些快炒店甚至提供火鍋。

C It usually has at least 20 to 30 dishes. I used to live in a house in downtown Tainan and three houses down was a stir fry store. I ate there all the time. I usually ordered a bowl of rice, two stir fry vegetables and soup meat.

通常快炒店會有至少 20 到 30 道菜可以點。我以前住的房子在台南市中心，隔三間房子就是一家快炒店。我常常去吃。我通常會點一碗飯、兩道炒蔬菜，還有一碗肉湯。

Information 美食報馬仔

　　赤崁樓附近的石精臼有很多經典的傳統小吃，像是米糕、鹹粥、鴨肉羹、海產粥、擔仔麵、肉粽、碗粿、浮水花枝羹、肉圓、滷味和冬瓜茶等等。赤崁樓附近還有祀典武廟與大天后可以拜拜祈求平安順利。祀典武廟前有古早味的義豐冬瓜茶。還有創立於 1975 年的武廟肉圓，武廟肉圓是用清蒸的方式，清蒸肉圓清爽不油膩，肉圓還附有一碗有加柴魚末與芹菜的大骨湯！

Unit 23
Tainan
Salty porridge
台南－鹹粥

 Attractions 景點報報

台南孔廟是國家一級古蹟，也是台灣第一次舉行祭孔典禮的地方，從後門走出去會看到了一棟很漂亮的建築物叫武德殿。孔廟正門對面是永華宮，離孔廟不遠處就是國立台灣文學館。台南孔廟前的府前路以及附近的南門路是吃吃逛逛的好地方。客林的八寶肉包和香菇水晶餃是道地的古早味。附近的莉莉水果店、福記肉圓、阿川土魠魚羹都是有名的小吃。孔廟對面的府中街可以吃到人氣很旺的保哥黑輪和炒泡麵。

Popular snacks / street food 人氣小吃報報

Salty porridge is a classic southern Taiwan breakfast dish, enjoyed with gusto – and a fried donut stick – in Tainan. The rice and broth for this salty porridge are prepared so that the rice remains light and firm. In the common rice congee, the rice is cooked with large amounts of water long enough to make the grains so soft that they begin to break apart. Salty porridge in Tainan is made so that the clear fish broth is added over the cooked rice, seafood and any vegetables at the end of cooking. And the main ingredient of salty porridge is milkfish – a popular, mild-tasting white fish. There are many other ways that milkfish is enjoyed in Tainan – in soup, fried, and as fish balls, for example. Most Milkfish available in Taiwan is not wild-caught, but raised through aquaculture or fish farming systems. Traditionally, the fish fingerlings are caught in the open sea, then raised in ponds or under-water cages of warm, brackish coastal water. Production of milkfish in Southeast Asia using this method has increased nearly 1,000 times since 1950. The Philippines and Indonesia join Taiwan as the top milkfish producers and consumers.

 中譯

　　鹹粥是一種典型的台灣南部早餐，加上油條味道就很棒。做鹹粥的米要煮到軟且粒粒分明。就一般煮粥的方式，米會加大量的水煮足夠長的時間，使米粒軟到開始分解。台南鹹粥則是把清澈魚湯加在米飯上，在烹煮最後加入海鮮和蔬菜。鹹粥的主要成分是虱目魚，這是一種很受歡迎吃起來軟嫩的魚。在台南虱目魚的吃法還有許多方式，做湯、用煎的，或做成魚丸。在台灣吃的虱目魚大部分都不是野生捕撈的，而是由養殖或養魚系統。傳統上，魚苗是在大海捕獲的，然後養在池塘或靠近沿海溫度較暖和的鹹水魚塭內。自 1950 年在東南亞用這種方法養殖虱目魚產量就增加了近 1000 倍。菲律賓和印尼加入台灣成為主要的虱目魚生產者和消費者。

北台灣的文化風情 **1**

中台灣的魅力風情 **2**

南台灣的熱力風情 **3**

東台灣農村風情 **4**

Q & A 外國人都是這樣問 🔊 *MP3 23*

Q1 **Milkfish is not a familiar type of fish to me. What does it taste like?**
我對虱目魚不是很了解。吃起來是什麼口感？

A Milkfish is the most-consumed fish in Taiwan. The taste depends on how it is cooked and which part of the fish is cooked. Fresh fish is the key. If cooked right, fish skin and fish intestine are crunchy. Fish liver is very soft. Braised Milkfish head is also very tasty.

虱目魚是台灣人最常吃的魚。口感的話要看你怎麼煮，還有煮哪個部位。重點是魚一定要新鮮。如果煮得好的話，魚皮吃起來就脆脆的。魚肝吃起來非常軟嫩。滷虱目魚魚頭也是很美味。

B You might think it tastes like cod or scrod. I think it's just a very soft meat with a mild flavor, but full of important nutrients for good health.

你可能會覺得它的味道像鱈魚或小鱈魚。我認為這只是一個很軟的肉，味道也很溫和，但含有很多讓身體健康的重要營養物質。

C Milkfish is a local saltwater fish. Fish farmers raise most of the milkfish available today, insuring good quality mild-tasting fish.

虱目魚是當地的海水魚。現在的虱目魚都是魚民養殖，這樣可以確保養出肉質好、味道溫和的魚。

A The toppings could vary depending on the shop where you buy the porridge or what a family's taste might be. Very commonly though, you will find fresh green onion and cilantro leaves, dried pork threads, fried shallots, soy sauce, chili oil, and sesame oil.

粥上面的配料會因為賣家的不同，或者各個家庭喜歡的味道而有不同。比較普遍放的通常是新鮮的蔥和香菜、豬鬆、爆紅蔥頭、醬油、辣椒油與香油。

B The common toppings are chopped green onion or diced celery or even cilantro. Some people like to add extra soy sauce and sesame oil. Some add fried garlic and cilantro.

常見的配料是蔥花或切細的芹菜，甚至是香菜。有些人喜歡添加額外的醬油和香油。也有的會加蒜頭酥與香菜。

C Youtiao is the best topping. I love that fried pastry stick. I was told there is a good reason to eat Youtiao with milkfish porridge. There are many small bones in milkfish and sometimes a bone might scratch your throat. The smooth and greasy Youtiao can help ease the scratch.

油條是最棒的配料。我很喜歡。有人跟我說吃虱目魚粥為何要配油條的理由，原來，虱目魚的魚刺很多，有時不小心會被魚刺鯁到，滑滑油油的油條是用來舒緩鯁刺感。

Are there other seafoods in the salty porridge besides milkfish?

鹹粥裡除了虱目魚以外通常還會加海鮮嗎？

A Yes, the most popular vendors also include oysters.

是的，很多人氣高的商家會加蚵仔。

B Many times there can be other types of seafood, yes. The great thing about eating the salty porridge in Tainan is how fresh the seafood is. The cook bought freshly caught or harvested seafood early enough this morning to prepare the stock and serve the porridge fresh to her 6 a.m. customers!

是的，很多時候會加其他類型的海鮮。在台南吃鹹粥最棒的就是海鮮的新鮮。通常是商家買當天早上捕獲或收穫的海鮮後，馬上用來煮粥讓清晨六點的客人可以吃得到！

C Milkfish will be the most abundant seafood in any salty porridge, partly because Tainan people love it so much, but also because it is less expensive than many other types of seafood. So, there may be a taste of oyster or some other shellfish, but milkfish is still the primary ingredient.

虱目魚是鹹粥裡最常放的海鮮，部分是因為台南人很愛這個味道，還有這種魚比其他類型的海鮮便宜。因此，鹹粥是有可能加蚵仔或其他一些貝類，但虱目魚仍然是主要食材。

Information 美食報馬仔

鹹粥古早味是在台南不容錯過好滋味的平民小吃，這些店的特色都是採用當日新鮮的虱目魚、阿憨鹹粥、阿月虱目魚、阿堂鹹粥、悅津鹹粥和阿星鹹粥，都是很受歡迎的鹹粥店家。這些店的虱目魚料理其實都大同小異也都十分平價，主要虱目魚肉質都很鮮甜，新鮮就是品質保證。滷虱目魚頭、海產粥、魚肚湯、肉燥飯、虱目魚粥、煎魚肚、乾燙魚腸和蝦仁飯都是一般鹹粥店提供的菜單。

Unit 24
Tainan
local beef
台南－土產牛肉

 Attractions 景點報報

很多台南人會把牛肉湯當早餐。這種牛肉的主要特色是溫體牛肉，也就是當天新鮮現宰，尚未進過冰箱的牛肉。臺南大部分的牛肉小吃店的溫體牛就是來自善化的牛肉屠宰場。善化牛墟是台灣目前僅存的三大牛墟之一（北港、鹽水與善化）。牛墟就是牛隻買賣交易的地方，因為人潮的聚集所以漸漸形成買賣牛具、農具、衣服或小吃的市集。逛善化牛墟的樂趣就好像同時逛大型的菜市場和夜市。

 Popular snacks / street food 人氣小吃報報

Tainan's famous beef soup a clear beef broth with Chinese herbs, poured boiling hot over raw pieces of thinly sliced beef. The heat of the soup cooks the beef as the vendor serves it. The best beef soup to be found on Tainan's streets uses local beef that comes fresh daily from the beef cattle farms near Tainan. Butchering occurs twice a day, once in the morning and once at night, in Shan Hua Tainan. This allows for the freshly butchered beef to be delivered directly to soup shops in the heart of the city and served as fresh as possible. Unlike western beef that is frozen right after butchering, Shan Hua Cattle Market provides "body temperature beef" which is cut beef that involves no freezing process and the meat structural integrity is not destroyed. Beef is cut and soon delivered to the market. It is said that only "body temperature beef" can be used for the best result for Tainan beef soup. Beef farming is not a large industry in Taiwan and the domestic beef is exclusively for local restaurants. Beef is becoming more available for household cooking with French retailer Carefree and American retailer Costo selling their beef imported from Australia or the US.

 中譯

　　台南著名的牛肉湯湯頭是中藥熬煮的清湯，滾燙的清湯，再倒入切得超薄的牛肉就可以上桌了。湯頭的熱度在上桌的同時會把牛肉幾乎燙熟。在台南最好的牛肉湯，是用每天來自台南附近養殖場的本地牛肉。台南善化牛墟，一天屠宰牛隻兩次，分別在上午和晚上，這樣可以讓新鮮屠宰的牛肉被直接送至各城市的小吃店，小吃店所提供的牛肉也就越新鮮越好。不像西方牛肉通常是在屠宰後立即冷凍，善化牛墟提供的是「溫體牛」，就是現殺，沒經過冷藏，肉質結構完整沒被破壞的，溫體牛在屠宰後很快就被供應到市場。有人說，只有「體溫牛」才能做出最棒的台南牛肉湯。牛肉養殖在台灣不是一個大產業，國內的牛肉是專門賣給小吃店。來自法國大賣場的家樂福和美國大賣場的好市多所賣的牛肉是澳大利亞和美國進口的，這樣一般家庭就比較容易買到牛肉。

Q & A 外國人都是這樣問 🔊 *MP3 24*

Q1 **How is beef noodle soup different from beef soup in Tainan?**
一般的牛肉麵跟台南的牛肉湯當有什麼不一樣呢？

A One has no noodles. People eat beef noodle soup for lunch or dinner. Beef soup in Tainan is mostly for breakfast with rice.

一種是沒有加麵。通常牛肉麵是午餐或晚餐會吃。台南的牛肉湯是當早餐配飯吃。

B The beef soup in Tainan focuses on the beef's fresh, quick cooking. Beef is sliced very thin, just add hot broth and it is ready to serve. Beef is still slightly raw. It is soft and melts in your mouth. The beef noodle soup is a much slower preparation where the beef braises in the broth for hours before serving.

台南的牛肉湯頭是重在牛肉的新鮮度，牛肉切薄片放入碗內，吃的時候才把高湯淋上，牛肉還微帶有血絲，不過超柔軟好吃的

啦，有點入口即化。一般的牛肉麵的湯頭與肉都是熬煮多個小時的。

C Tainan beef soup is a really simple, unique Taiwanese dish, served with a side of rice. The broth is clear. Beef noodle soup has vegetables and noodles. The broth usually has dark color because of soy sauce, oyster sauce and fermented bean sauce are added.

台南牛肉湯是非常簡單的湯，有很獨特的台灣味，吃的時候配碗飯。湯是比較清的湯。一般的牛肉麵會加蔬菜還有麵條，湯頭的顏色也比較深，因為有加醬油、蠔油和豆瓣醬。

1 北台灣的文化風情

2 中台灣的魅力風情

3 南台灣的熱力風情

4 東台灣農村風情

Q2 What type of menu does the beef vendor usually offer?

通常牛肉店的菜單都有什麼呢？

A Beef fried rice, beef risotto, beef liver with sesame oil, sesame beef, scallion beef, Chinese kale stir fried with beef, cabbage with beef, beef mixed soup, veggie with beef or even beef jerky.

牛肉炒飯、牛肉燴飯、麻油心肝、麻油牛肉、蔥爆牛肉、芥藍牛肉、高麗菜牛腩、牛雜湯、青菜炒牛肉，甚至也會賣牛肉乾。

B They often offer stir fried vegetables without meat. Most dishes are beef based so stir fried vegetables seem exceptionally tasty with other beef dishes. You can order stir fried vegetables with beef as well, such as cabbage stir fry with beef or Chinese kale stir fry with beef are common on the menu.

他們通常也會有炒青菜，因為太多肉，所以炒青菜吃起來似乎格外爽口。當然你也可以點牛肉炒青菜。像是高麗菜炒牛肉或芥藍

炒牛肉也都是菜單上常見的。

C They usually have different beef based soups. My favorite is beef mixed soup. "Mixed" here means using different parts of beef internal organs in broth, and cook with ginger, onion, and other Chinese herbs. I also like white radish beef soup. When white radish is in season, it is so sweet and is best in soup. Beef kidney soup is also good. It's soft and crunchy. Amazing !

通常會提供不同湯頭的選項。我最喜歡的是牛雜湯。「牛雜」指的是牛的其他內臟熬上幾個小時用薑母、洋蔥與中藥所熬煮的湯。我也喜歡菜頭牛肉湯，菜頭是當季吃起來很甜，整碗湯也相當的甘甜好喝。還有牛肉腰子湯真的是很不錯。腰子超級軟，口感 Q 彈，真的太好喝了！

1 北台灣的文化風情

2 中台灣的魅力風情

3 南台灣的熱力風情

4 東台灣農村風情

Q3 Can the hot broth really cook the beef that quickly?

這種熱湯真的可以很快地把牛肉煮好嗎？

A Yes, because the beef is sliced so thinly, and the broth is boiling hot when ladled over the beef strips.

是的。因為牛肉切得很薄，熱騰騰的大骨高湯淋上後，隨即就能端上桌。

B Remember that these are the best cuts of beef, so even if the meat is still a little pink when eaten, it is perfectly safe.

這樣的牛肉通常是部位最好的現切牛肉，所以就算肉色還有一點粉紅，也是安全可以吃的。

C It's not a problem at all. Have you ever eaten Vietnamese beef pho? The beef in that soup is also cooked when the hot broth pours over the top.

沒問題的。你有聽過越南牛肉麵嗎？也是用湯頭淋在牛肉片上的。

 ## *Information* 美食報馬仔

台南到處可以看到賣牛肉湯的小吃店。安平地區三大牛肉湯都在安平古堡街上，分別為文章牛肉湯、助仔牛肉湯，以及位在三級古蹟妙壽宮旁邊的阿財牛肉湯，大灣有鴻品牛肉，小北有榮吉炒牛肉，長榮路一段有長榮牛肉湯，台南市海安路有六千牛肉湯，善化區有阿春土產牛肉，下營鄉有意林牛肉湯。無論在台南任何時間的那一區，都可以吃到屬於台南味道的新鮮牛肉湯。

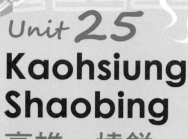

Unit 25
Kaohsiung Shaobing
高雄－燒餅

 Attractions 景點報報

左營是軍事重地，也是不同文化融合的古城。夏天的蓮池潭可以欣賞蓮花與荷花，蓮池潭東岸是左營蓮池潭自行車道，沿途可見古色古香的廟宇以及美麗的池潭，西岸為左營的舊市街，在地人都知道在安靜的巷弄裡隱藏眷村傳統美食。當地廟宇的宗教慶典活動是在每年十月中旬的「萬年季」，左營是台灣寺廟最集中的地方。左營的新孔廟位於左營蓮池潭北岸，是台灣最大的孔廟。

 Popular snacks / street food 人氣小吃報報

Shaobing, or Chinese flat bread is a flaky, tasty flat bread popular throughout Taiwan. One of the breakfast choices in Taiwan is shaobing wrapped around the airy fried dough stick known as Chinese cruller or Youtiao, plus a bowl of warm soy milk. The origin of shaobing is probably in the north of China, since it uses wheat flour. However, shaobing in Taiwan is a part of military history. When Chiang Kai-shek brought his Chinese troops to Taiwan, his government built housing compounds for his military families all over the western coastline of Taiwan waiting to eventually go back to their motherland China. Zuo Ying in the southern port city of Kaohsiung was an important naval base and Chiang Kai-shek's government built more than 20 military family compounds. They started making their own food and sold it in the street. Many people in Taiwan who were students in the 60's or 70's have memories of buying or seeing mainlanders selling their traditional food in the streets near schools. Shaobing is one of the foods starting out this way and then making it to mainstream food in Taiwan.

 中譯

　　燒餅是一種中式的酥脆麵包，這種美味的燒餅在整個台灣都很流行。其中一種在台灣的早餐吃法就是燒餅油條加上一碗溫豆漿。燒餅很可能是起源於中國北方，因為是使用小麥粉。不過，燒餅在台灣也是軍隊歷史的一部分。當蔣介石帶著他的中國軍隊到台灣，他的政府就沿著西部海岸線各地為他的軍人和他們的家人建蓋眷村，最終是要等待回到自己的中國祖國。左營是當時重要海軍基地，蔣介石政府就在左營蓋了 20 幾個眷村。眷村的人也開始製作自己家鄉的食物賣給眷村外街上的人。許多在台灣六、七年級生於學生時期都會有印象會看到外省伯伯在學校附近賣自己的家鄉食物。燒餅就是這樣的食物之一，並成了台灣的主流食物。

Q1 **How does the shaobing become so flaky and crispy?**
燒餅是怎麼做得酥酥脆脆的呢？

A It's so delicious, isn't it? This is truly the art of bread baking. The basic ingredients are flour, salt, oil, hot water and cold water. What could be more simple than that? It is also critical how each ingredient is added. Hot water has to be added first, for example.

真的很好吃，對嗎？這其實是一門烘烤的藝術。基本材料只是麵粉、鹽、油、熱水和冷水。還有什麼比這更簡單的呢？重要的是每種食材是如何的和在一起的。比如必須先加熱水。

B Roux is used in the process. Flour has to low heat fry until golden brown. Let it cool and then it is used to spread onto the rolled out dough. The baker then folds it together and rolls it out again before baking.

這是有加油酥的關係。麵粉必須用小火慢炒至金黃褐色，放涼備用。把油酥均勻塗抹於麵皮上，做成小麵糰和在一起，桿開後烘培。

〜〜〜〜〜〜〜〜〜〜〜〜〜〜〜〜〜〜〜〜〜〜

C Does the flakiness remind you of French croissant? The baker folds in a layer of vegetable oil or fat in somewhat the same way that a French baker folds in butter. Then of course, it must be baked properly.

那種酥酥脆脆的的口感是不是很像法國羊角麵包呢？油酥加入麵團的做法很像法國麵包把奶油加入麵團摺疊起一樣。當然，烘烤也一定要控制好才行。

A In Taiwan, shaobing is essential on the breakfast table. This dish that was usually made with shaobing wrapped around airy fried dough stick, known as Chinese cruller, or youtiao -- plus a bowl of warm soy milk -- has become a new fashion nowadays. It can be served with other breakfast foods, such as bacon and eggs. The most popular way to eat shaobing is for breakfast with youtiao wrapped inside.

在台灣,燒餅在早餐餐桌上是不可或缺的。這個餐點通常製成,由燒餅捲著油條,或稱作油炸小煎餅,另外再加上溫暖的豆漿,已成了現今的新流行。它能與其他食物搭著吃,例如培根和蛋。燒餅加油條是很普遍的吃法。

B I like it for breakfast with fried egg mixed with green onion.

我喜歡燒餅加蔥蛋。

C I like shaobing deluxe style. I like it with an egg and a slice of ham. You can have it with just an egg. Or you can have it with youtiao. There is also shaobing with hot dog. What sounds good to you today? All go well with hot soy milk.

我喜歡豪華版的燒餅，裡面有加火腿和蛋。你也可以只加荷包蛋或者就吃燒餅油條，也有燒餅夾熱狗。你今天想要吃哪一種？這些和熱豆漿很配。

1 北台灣的文化風情

2 中台灣的魅力風情

3 南台灣的熱力風情

4 東台灣農村風情

Q3 Does a shaobing vendor only sell one item or something more?

一般賣燒餅的都只有賣一種品項？還是有其他？

A It depends. A street vendor that sells shaobing for afternoon snack might only sell shaobing with different choices of fillings.

看情況。如果攤販只是賣下午點心的，通常會只賣燒餅，但會提供不同加料。

B If it is a traditional breakfast shop, it usually sells lots of items in addition to shaobing. The classic items are steamed bun, flat bread with egg, youtiao, fried meat bun, fried vegetable bun, fried dumplings, toast and egg.

如果是傳統早餐店，通常除了燒餅 以外，店家還會賣很多其他品項。經典品項會有饅頭、蛋餅、油條、煎肉包、煎餃、土司和荷包蛋。

C The breakfast shop near my house does not have good shaobing. They don't make it themselves. They sell many other items such as stuffed rice, flatbread with egg and steamed white radish cake. Their stuffed rice is the best. It has egg, dried meat, spicy dried radish and youtiao.

我們家附近那家的燒餅油條不好吃，不是自己現做的，但是他們還有賣飯糰，蛋餅還有蘿蔔糕。他們的飯糰比什麼都好吃，裡面只是加蛋、肉鬆、辣菜脯及油條。

 ## *Information* 美食報馬仔

　　位於高雄六合二路上的興隆居傳統早餐店創立於 1954 年，提供煎包、煎餃、菜包、脆皮鍋貼、饅頭、飯糰、蛋餅、燒餅、油條還有湯包等，傳統手工現做加上口味多樣化讓食客有很多選擇。海青王家燒餅賣的是現桿現製的燒餅外皮脆、內 Q 軟，燒餅內可加酸黃瓜、酸菜、豆乾或柞菜、燒餅夾蛋菜、招牌燒餅、燒餅夾黑輪蛋菜，總匯燒餅加上自製的小菜及辣醬都是吃燒餅的多樣變化選擇。

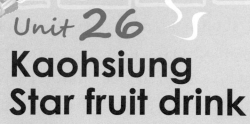

Unit 26
Kaohsiung
Star fruit drink
高雄－楊桃湯

Attractions 景點報報

高雄西子灣有美麗的港灣和沙灘，國立中山大學就在西子灣風景區，這是台灣唯一依山傍海擁有海灘的大學，校內還有全長約 1.5 公里的南壽山環境教育步道。校區附近有古蹟雄鎮北門，這是已有三百年歷史的國家三級古蹟，是小型砲臺的城門。前清打狗英國領事館建於 1800 年末期至今已有 140 年歷史，屬二級古蹟，這裡可以看西子灣日落以及高雄市港全景，目前是私人企業經營咖啡館，但有開放遊客參觀古蹟。

Popular snacks / street food 人氣小吃報報

Star fruit – also known as carambola – is a sweet and juicy tropical fruit with five distinct ridges running its length. Carambola's roots branches, leaves, flowers, and fruits all can be used for medicinal purposes. Carambola contains sucrose, fructose, glucose, malic acid, citric acid, oxalic acid and vitamins B1, B2, C and protein. In ancient times, it was used for its antibiotic effect to fight malaria. Star fruit in Taiwan is commonly used for sore throat. Turning the fruit into fermented juice is as simple as combining equal parts sliced fruit and sugar in a large jar, covering it to keep the insects out, and setting the jar in the sun for a few days. Alcohol content would increase to the level of a fruit wine if the jar was left for a full three weeks. Vendors serve up the fermented drink up ice cold in plastic to-go cups with straws. Fermented star fruit drink can also be served hot. In addition to ready to serve cold star fruit drink, vendors also sell concentrated star fruit drink in bottles. In winter people like to add hot water to the star fruit drink concentrate.

 中譯

　　楊桃是一種五角形的、甜美多汁的熱帶水果。楊桃的根、枝、葉、花、果都有藥用性質。楊桃含有蔗糖、果糖、葡萄糖、蘋果酸、檸檬酸、草酸、維生素 B1、B2、C 及蛋白質。在古代，楊桃的抗生素效果被用來對抗瘧疾。在台灣楊桃常用於治咽喉腫痛。楊桃汁是由發酵過的楊桃所做的，發酵的楊桃做法很簡單，楊桃切片後每一層撒上糖放入一個大罐子，蓋起來防止害蟲入侵，放在太陽下幾天就完成了。如果放滿三星期，楊桃發酵後的酒精含量就能釀成水果酒。攤販賣的楊桃湯通常會把冰冷的楊桃湯倒入塑料外帶杯裝的吸管。楊桃湯也可以做熱飲。一般攤販除了賣馬上可以喝的冰楊桃湯，他們也會賣瓶裝的濃縮楊桃湯。冬天很多人喜歡買濃縮的楊桃湯回家自己加熱水。

Q1 How does the star fruit tree grow anyway?
楊桃樹是怎麼生長的呢?

Ⓐ It grows on trees with glossy green leaves. The height of the tree is about 10 meters.

楊桃樹是屬於綠性灌木。樹高可達 10 餘公尺。

Ⓑ On trees like citrus, though the whole fruit does not look like a star. The star can't be seen unless you slice the fruit across its five deep ridges.

很像柑橘樹,雖然整個水果看起來並不像星星狀,但橫切水果的五脊片就能看得出來。

Ⓒ The star fruit eaten here was probably grown on a tree farm in Taiwan, but the tree is native to more tropical areas of Asia such as the Philippines, Indonesia, Vietnam, India, and Sri Lanka.

台灣的楊桃應該都是生長在果園裡，但樹種原產於亞洲較熱帶地區，如菲律賓、印尼、越南、印度和斯里蘭卡。

How much of this fermented drink would a person be able to consume without becoming intoxicated?

這種發酵飲料要喝多少才會讓人有醉意?

A People have a craze for star fruit drinks, knowing that it contains several key vitamins that are vital to our health. Customers might drink like a dozen in a week. We know what nutrients star fruits contain, and we know the benefit of drinking it, but we don't have a clear idea about star fruits. The fermentation might bring very little alcohol content but it is the sourness that make this drink wonderful. It is totally diluted with water so no one thinks of it having alcohol content.

人們對楊桃汁有著狂熱,知道它所含的幾個關鍵維他命對我們的健康是重要的。顧客可能會一周喝個 12 杯。我們知道楊桃汁所含的營養成分。我們知道喝這個的好處,但是我們對楊桃本身沒有很清楚的認識。發酵可能會帶來非常少的酒精含量,但是發酵後的酸味很棒。發酵後的楊桃汁是加很多水稀釋,所以不會覺得有酒精含量。

B Are you joking? Intoxicated? I don't think so. Star fruit drink is a very common street drink in Taiwan. It is like buying a cup of cold tea. Star fruit drink brings cold, sour and sweet to the taste buds, throat, and stomach and spreads the feeling to the whole body. This is the charm of a cold cup of star fruit drink in the hot summer.

你在開玩笑嗎？酒精？我不認為。楊桃汁在台灣是很普遍的飲料，就好像在街上買一杯冰茶一樣。楊桃汁那種冰涼酸甜的感覺會從味蕾、喉嚨沁涼到胃，在蔓延至全身，這就是楊桃湯在炎熱夏天的魅力。

C There is no such thing. Don't worry about being intoxicated with star fruit drink. It's good both ways, cold or hot. When I have a sorc throat, I drink a lot of warm star fruit drink. It is better than medicine. I like to add a little plum powder. It is so delicious.

沒這回事。不要擔心喝楊桃汁會醉。楊桃汁冷或熱都很好喝。當我喉嚨痛時，我都會喝很多溫溫的楊桃汁。這比藥更有效。我也喜歡加一點梅子粉，很棒。

Q3 Is all star fruit juice fermented?
楊桃汁都是發酵過的嗎？

A My friend told me that you can purchase unfermented canned star fruit juice throughout Asia. But, in Taiwan, I think it is all fermented.

我的朋友告訴我，你可以在亞洲很多地方可以買到未發酵的楊桃罐頭果汁。但是，在台灣，我覺得楊桃汁應該都是有發酵過的。

B At the street market, served in cups like this with a straw, it is all fermented and made in small batches.

在路上，商店賣的楊桃汁都是用有發酵過的楊桃做的，會像這樣裝在杯子裡用吸管喝。

C I never thought about this before. When star fruits are in season, we eat it fresh. We see star fruit drink vendors all year around. I assume it's all fermented. Maybe there is but I never heard of unfermented start fruit drink.

我從來沒有想過這個。當楊桃是當令水果時，我們都是吃新鮮楊桃。全年好像都可以看到攤販賣楊桃汁。我覺得應該都是發酵過的。也許有，但我從來沒有聽說過未發酵的楊桃汁。

 ## Information 美食報馬仔

冰涼酸甜的楊桃汁的魅力在炎熱的南台灣是無法擋的。在左營大路與店仔頂路交叉口的左營永吉楊桃湯已經經營 60 年了。永吉只賣一種價格的楊桃湯，在附近的龔家楊桃湯則有賣三種價位的楊桃湯。這兩家楊桃汁口味有微不同，皆有販售冷熱，這兩家也都有賣罐裝濃縮的楊桃汁，買回家後可以自行加入冰水或熱水，直接飲用。

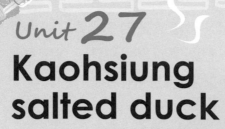

Unit 27
Kaohsiung salted duck
高雄－鹹水鴨

Attractions 景點報報

內惟埤文化園區位於高雄市鼓山區，是都會裡的森林園區，園區內有高雄市立美術館、兒童美術館與湖泊，也有戶外藝術品，步道路線，木橋、木造步道、石頭步道。高雄兒童美術館是台灣第一個以兒童為對象的公營美術館，館前有可玩的沙坑，大樹下的園地有腳印迷宮、藝術搖籃座椅。館內有可參觀、可動手、可玩的多元展覽。對大人小孩來說這裡是一個戶內戶外皆可玩遊戲、玩藝術的好地方。

Popular snacks / street food 人氣小吃報報

Salted duck tastes effortless and simple, though the Kaohsiung cooks who prepare it have several steps to follow in order to make it well. Its ingredients are simply duck, salt, pepper, ginger, green onion, and other spices. These are not hard to come by, so it is the various steps of marinating, cooking, and cooling that give the dish its traditional texture and taste. Traditional cooks may maintain the "starter broth" from previous salted duck cooking sessions to yield an even richer experience. Salted duck is a cold dish of sliced duck. Salted duck was originally a specialty of Nanjing, China, capital of the Qing Dynasty. The Qing emperor conquered and annexed Taiwan in the mid seventeenth century, ruling it for over two centuries. It's reasonable to assume that salted duck was brought to Taiwan from China. An amusing story from Nanjing attempts to explain how duck became so popular there centuries ago. Legend has it that a dispute about excess noise caused all the roosters to be killed. The result was no more noisy wake-up calls, but also no more chicken to eat. This is said to be the time period when the locals turned to duck as a source of protein.

 中譯

　　鹽水鴨吃起來是那麼輕鬆和簡單的味道，雖然簡單但是還是需要好幾個步驟才能做得出好吃的鹽水鴨。鹽水鴨的材料只是簡單的鴨、鹽、胡椒、姜、蔥和其他香料。這些材料都不難取得，透過醃製，烹調和冷卻的各個步驟，讓這道菜有很特別的傳統肉質和口感。有些廚師可能會保留煮過的鹽水鴨的高湯再加入煮新鹽水鴨，這樣可以讓味道更加豐富。鹽水鴨通常是切片的一道涼菜。鹽水鴨源自中國南京，是清朝首都的特產。清朝皇帝在十七世紀中期吞併台灣，統治了兩個多世紀。因此，可以合理的假設，台灣的鹽水鴨是源自中國。在南京有一個讓人莞爾一笑的說法，解釋為何鴨肉在那裡幾百年前這麼流行。傳說是過度噪音的糾紛導致所有的公雞被殺害。也因此早晨不會聽到吵醒居民的啼叫聲，但同時也沒有雞肉可以吃了。也就在那時，當地人把吃鴨肉作為蛋白質取得的來源。

Q1 **Duck is so fatty. Doesn't it taste too heavy?**
鴨肉有很多油脂，味道不會太重嗎？

A Actually, because the sauce and spices are so simple, the meat itself is really the star.

其實，因為醃的醬料與香料都是很簡單的食材，肉本身好吃才是重點。

B I think it might be too heavy if there was an extra added thick sauce or if the duck was deep-fat fried. This way it actually tastes light and fresh. When you buy a box of salted duck, the vendor usually gives you some duck soup base. It is very flavorful. You can drizzle a little on the top of the sliced duck meat. Or freeze it, add it in stir fry or make a soup with it.

我想如果有額外加濃郁的醬汁或鴨是有炸過的，這樣味道可能太重。鹽水鴨的做法實際上吃起來是很清淡和新鮮的。買鹹水鴨時，店家還會附了一包鴨湯，十分有風味，可以淋在鴨肉上面，可以先冷凍起來加入炒菜或高湯。

C Personally, I love it though I only eat a slice or two at a time. Please try some and see for yourself! After the duck is refrigerated, it is very chewy. Never heat it up.

就個人來說，我是很喜歡但一次只能吃幾片。你就試試看吧。鹽水鴨冰過之後很 Q，絕對不要加熱吃。

What spices are used to prepare this dish?
鹽水鴨的醃料是什麼呢？

A The dish uses what you may know as Chinese Five Spice: star anise, cinnamon, fennel, Sichuan pepper, and cumin. Ginger, green onions, salt, and licorice are also added.

這道菜用到的香料就是五香粉：八角、桂皮、茴香、花椒和小茴香。也會加入薑、蔥、鹽還有甘草。

B Salt and pepper are the stars of the show, but the cook adds traditional spices like star anise, cinnamon, fennel, Sichuan pepper, cumin and ginger.

鹽和胡椒是重點，但有些做法會加入傳統的香料，料像八角、桂皮、茴香、花椒、小茴香和薑。

C It really does not use too many spices. My mom used to make it with salt, rice wine, white peppers and sesame oil. The key procedure is to marinate it overnight. After it is cooked and cooled, refrigerate it for at least 3 hours. Save the broth for soup. You can cook the same thing with whole chicken. It is just as good.

其實不需要很多香料。我媽媽以前會用鹽、米酒、白胡椒粉、麻油來醃肉，重點是要放冰箱醃製一晚。用水煮熟鴨子後取出待涼，放進冰箱冷藏約 3 小時就可以切來吃。煮鴨的高湯可以留下來煮湯。你也可以用同樣的方式來做鹽水雞，也是很好吃。

Isn't duck so much more expensive than chicken?

鴨肉不會比雞肉貴嗎？

A Not in Taiwan. The prices of fresh, whole duck and chicken are about the same.

在台灣不會。鴨和雞的價格其實差不多。

B No, because duck is so popular in Taiwan that there are plenty of duck farmers to help keep supplies high. There is a Duck Research Center in I-Lan.

不會，因為鴨肉在台灣很受歡迎，所以有很多養鴨的農民，以保持充足的肉源。台灣還有一個養鴨研究中心，就在宜蘭。

C No, duck is not more expensive than chicken – not really. Is duck more expensive in your country?

不會，鴨肉並會比雞肉更貴，真的不會。在你的國家鴨肉是比較貴嗎？

 Information 美食報馬仔

高雄市左營區左營蘇家鹹水鴨屬於南京鹹水鴨的做法，吃過的人都會説那是令人忘不了的好吃味道。他們會接受訂購與團購，蘇家鹹水鴨就只賣鹹水鴨。在左營有 50 餘年的陳家鹽水鴨賣的是鹽水鴨還有香酥鴨。香酥鴨是鹽水鴨炸過之後再加上檸檬汁或特製蜜汁就變成了外皮酥脆、有特殊口味的香酥鴨，除了鹽水鴨與香酥鴨之外，陳家還有賣許多種不同口味的滷味。

Unit 28
Pingtung
Pepper shrimp
屏東—胡椒蝦

 Attractions 景點報報

　　屏東「六堆客家文化園區」離屏東市很近，這是由六個碟子型屋頂構成，有部落聚集的意義。六堆是指聚居高屏地區的客家人，「堆」是聚集也是「隊」的意思，「六堆」指的是客家人發起六隊義兵來保衛家鄉。園區裡除了有客家文物館外還有池塘與菸樓，也有童趣與鄉間味道的兒童探索區與沙堆，遊客可以感受別具一格的客家文化，飲食、想法與生活方式。

 Popular snacks / street food 人氣小吃報報

In many tropical, coastal areas of the world, shrimp is a staple food. Cultivating shrimp in small agricultural settings goes back to at least the 15th century in southeast Asia. Taiwan was an early adopter of fish farming on an industrial scale in the southern part of the island and quickly became one of the largest suppliers of exported shrimp. Sadly, the industry and the environment suffered great losses due to unsustainable practices during the 1980s. Since shrimp are relatively easy to grow and need only six months to mature from an egg to an adult shrimp, it's not surprising that shrimp is an ingredient in many traditional dishes in Taiwan. Taiwanese believe that shrimp are the sweetest when cooked in the shell. Among the dishes you may encounter in Taiwan are shrimp ball soup, shrimp in braised cabbage or stir-fried noodles, and pepper shrimp. Pepper shrimp is a relatively simple dish, made by soaking the whole unpeeled shrimp in rice wine, lightly breading it to deep fry it and then tossing in a pan for a quick stir fry with oil, garlic, ginger, and other spices. The shrimp is then arranged beautifully on a plate to be shared.

 ## 中譯

　　在世界許多熱帶沿海地區，蝦是一種主食。在東南亞小型的蝦養殖可以追溯到至少 15 世紀。台灣是最早在南部以產業規模做蝦養殖，並迅速成為出口蝦的最大供應商之一。不幸的是，在 80 年代期間的產業和環境，因為不當做法而遭受巨大損失。由於蝦是相對容易生長，由蝦卵到成蝦的成熟只需要六個月的成長期，所以在台灣許多傳統菜餚把蝦當作食材並不奇怪。台灣人認為，帶殼煮蝦最能煮出蝦的甜味。在台灣會常看到的蝦料理有蝦丸湯、麻油蝦、炒麵加蝦和胡椒蝦。胡椒蝦是很簡單的一道菜，把未去皮的蝦浸泡在米酒裡，輕輕裹上麵包屑後炸到金黃，撈起後在鍋裡加油和大蒜、生薑等香料快速翻炒就是一道簡單的胡椒蝦。出菜時，胡椒蝦漂亮地被鋪排在盤子上。

Q1 **Why don't the cooks remove the head, shell and legs – the exoskeleton – of the shrimp prior to cooking?**
為什麼廚師在料理前不把頭、外殼和腿都先去掉呢？

A I'm sorry for the inconvenience, but really the shrimp tastes so much sweeter if it is cooked with these parts intact. If you don't like it, just try something else. I understand that popping off the head and peeling off the legs at the table might be disgusting to westerners.

真是抱歉這樣讓你覺得不方便。但是，這樣烹煮的蝦才能保持蝦的甜味。如果你不喜歡，就吃別的。我知道對很多西方人來說，在桌上看到蝦頭，還有蝦腳會感到噁心。

B The freshest shrimps are cooked with the head, shell and legs in Taiwan. Only leftover shrimp or not-so-fresh shrimp are de-shelled. This assures you that this is the freshest shrimp you can get.

在台灣只有最新鮮的蝦才能整隻用來煮，包括頭、外殼和蝦腳。只有吃剩的蝦或不那麼新鮮的蝦才會去殼。帶殼的蝦才是新鮮的保證。

C Once you do it a few times and taste the delicious shrimp inside, you won't mind the work or be sickened by the process at all. Believe me, it is so worth it! Westerners' love for chicken fillet, fish fillet, de-shelled shrimp really says something about their culture. They can't stand it when cooking seems too barbaric.

你就不會介意蝦殼，或覺得過程很噁心。一旦你吃過幾次，也品嚐過蝦殼內的鮮美的味道，你就不會介意蝦殼或覺得撥蝦過程很噁心。相信我，這是很值得！西方人喜歡的雞排、魚排、無殼蝦都說明了他們的文化。他們無法忍受野蠻的煮法。

1 北台灣的文化風情

2 中台灣的魅力風情

3 南台灣的熱力風情

4 東台灣農村風情

Q2 Is this wild caught shrimp or farm-raised??
通常吃的蝦子是野生捕獲的還是養殖的?

A It must be farm-raised, since catching enough shrimp to meet the demand would be nearly impossible. We love shrimp too much and the ocean would soon be empty if we tried to only eat shrimp from the wild!

一定是人工養殖的,因為蝦的產量要滿足需求幾乎不可能。我們太喜歡吃蝦,如果只從野外捕獲蝦,那樣海洋很快就空空的了!

B Certainly farm-raised shrimps are more practical, abundant, and inexpensive. In several gourmet TV programs, there is an introduction about seafood, since the presenter knows how much people like it or value the nutrients it provides. They also reveal secrets about seafood, especially the level of freshness. Crabs and shrimps are often seen in the show. They tell you whether it is a wild shrimp or a farm-raised shrimp.

當然是養殖蝦,這樣比較實際、豐盛,而且價格也比較便宜。在幾個美食節目中,有著對海產的介紹,因為你知道大家多重視海產所含的營養成分。他們也揭露海產的秘密,像是新鮮的程度。

能在節目中常看到螃蟹和蝦子。他們告訴你這是野生捕獲的或是養殖的。

〰〰〰〰〰〰〰〰〰〰〰〰〰〰〰〰〰〰

C If it were wild caught, the sign would say so. Otherwise, everything is farm-raised.

如果是野生捕撈，應該會註明。否則，全都是養殖的。

Q3 What's your favorite shrimp dish?
你最喜歡的蝦料理是什麼？

A Peppered shrimp is my favorite. It is marinated with sea salt and a mix of white and black pepper. Ginger, garlic, and red chili peppers are the spices in this dish.

我最喜歡的是椒鹽蝦。這主是用海鹽以及特調椒鹽粉調味而成，也搭配了許多薑、蒜及辣椒。

B My favorite is shrimp fried with sesame oil and ginger.

我最喜歡的是麻油蝦，是用薑和麻油一起快炒的。

C I like them all. Sweet and sour shrimp has the sour and spicy sauce. Lemon shrimp has lemon juice and plum powder. It is very refreshing. I also like hot pot with lots of shrimp. I had a hot pot dish called mushroom health pot. There were so many types of mushrooms on the top and big shrimp underneath the mushrooms. The soup base had a little Chinese herbal flavor. It was delicious.

我都喜歡。酸辣蝦有加酸辣醬汁。檸檬蝦裡有檸檬汁及梅粉，吃起來很清爽。我也喜歡有很多蝦的火鍋。我吃過鮮菇養生鍋，鍋湯上浮著各種鮮菇，裡面有很多大蝦，湯頭還有淡淡的中藥味，真的好吃。

 ## *Information* 美食報馬仔

位於屏東縣林邊鄉中林路的水月軒雖在偏遠地方但常常座無虛席，這裡不止以鮮蝦料理聞名，庭園式詩情畫意的餐廳讓人彷彿走在詩境裡。這裡有湖、亭造景、小橋流水彷彿古代建築，十分古意盎然，小河裡有睡蓮，紅磚瓦的廁所也是特點。餐桌椅都是木桌木椅，非常古早味，水月軒賣的東西有火鍋、蝦料理、熱炒菜這三大類，必點料理是檸檬蝦、蒜泥蝦、鹽焗蝦、胡椒蝦還有櫻花蝦麵線。

1 北台灣的文化風情

2 中台灣的魅力風情

3 南台灣的熱力風情

4 東台灣農村風情

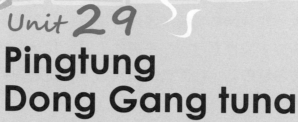

Unit 29
Pingtung
Dong Gang tuna
屏東－東港鮪魚

 ## *Attractions* 景點報報

　　屏東大鵬灣位在屏東縣東港鎮與林邊鄉交界處，是台灣最大的內灣，大鵬灣國家風景區的環灣自行車道全長約 12K，這裡是騎車健身和認識紅樹林、水鳥的最佳場所，途中會經過南平海堤、濱灣公園、青洲濱海遊憩區、跨海大橋、紅樹林濕地、木棧橋，大潭濕地、左右岸濕地和崎峰濕地，也會看到軍史遺跡，代表地標是鐵塔、水塔、水上飛機觀景台。黃昏的大鵬灣很浪漫動人。

 ## *Popular snacks / street food* 人氣小吃報報

There is no better time to go to Dong Gang port in Pingtung than during the annual Blue Fin Tuna Cultural Festival. Every year from May to July, the visitor can find a major celebration of tuna, founded securely in Pingtung's coastal Dong Gang Township in this tropical, southern area of Taiwan. Pacific blue fin tuna is much sought after, especially in Taiwan and Japan, for high quality sushi and sashimi. The Taiwanese tuna catch used to go almost exclusively to Japan, where bidders still pay top dollar for the rights to serve the biggest and best of the catch. Now, "tuna fever" captures the entire island of Taiwan during the later spring and early summer timeframe. In Taiwan, blue fin tuna is often referred to as "black tuna," but it is the same fish. Sakura shrimp and salted oilfish eggs are also popular in Dong Gang. The growth period for Sakura shrimp runs from November to June in nearby the coastal waters of Dong Gang port. Sakura shrimp has red pigment and light-emitting organs. It is usually fried or dried. Oilfish's eggs are salted, pressed and dried. It is usually thin sliced and is eaten with garlic and raw white radish.

　　東港黑鮪魚文化觀光季是去屏東東港的好時機。每年 5 月至 7 月，在台灣這個熱帶南部地區的屏東沿海東港鎮遊客可以看到有關黑鮪魚主要慶祝活動。太平洋黑鮪魚有很高的市場需求，特別是在台灣和日本，因為可以用來做高品質的壽司和生魚片。台灣以前捕獲的鮪魚幾乎都是賣去日本，投標人會付最高的價錢來買到最大和最好的魚。「黑鮪魚熱潮」現在則在春季和初夏時間風靡台灣。在台灣，這樣的藍鰭金槍魚常常被稱為「黑鮪魚」。東港還有櫻花蝦、油魚子。櫻花蝦產期為每年 11 至翌年 6 月就在東港溪出海口附近。櫻花蝦全身佈滿紅色素及發光器，通常會乾製或炸酥。油魚子的卵鹽醃後晾乾，吃的時候切成薄片再配上蒜苗與白蘿蔔。

1 北台灣的文化風情

2 中台灣的魅力風情

3 南台灣的熱力風情

4 東台灣農村風情

Q & A 外國人都是這樣問 ⦿)) *MP3 29*

Q1 **What is the classic way to eat the fresh blue fin tuna catch in Pingtung County?**
在屏東傳統吃黑鮪魚的方式是什麼？

A Blue fin tuna is called the Rolls-Royce of fish. The most expensive part and the best is used for sashimi. It just melts in your mouth.

黑鮪魚被譽為魚肉中的勞斯萊，最貴也是最好吃的部分會被做成生魚片，入口即化。

B I think the best way is tuna steak cooked on an iron plate. Even though the fish is cooked all the way, the meat is still very soft. It is really good. I have heard of eating blue fin tuna 18 ways but I have never tried it before.

我覺得最好吃的是鐵板松阪黑鮪魚，雖然在鐵板上煎得很熟，肉質還是很軟嫩，實在是太好吃了。我有聽過「黑鮪十八吃」但沒吃過。

C If it is fresh, it's all good. The fish chin is best for grilling. The fish head is food for stew or steamed dishes.

如果是新鮮，什麼料理都很好吃。魚的下巴適合香烤，魚頭用來燉湯或清蒸都很不錯。

1 北台灣的文化風情

2 中台灣的魅力風情

3 南台灣的熱力風情

4 東台灣農村風情

Q2 What kind of seafood dishes do you usually order?

你最喜歡點的海鮮是什麼？

A I like raw fish very much. I usually order sashimi made with red bigeye fish, flounder and tuna if it is in season. Also, a seafood plate of uncooked shrimp, snail meat, abalone and blood cockle are delicious as well.

我喜歡吃生魚。我通常會點生魚片，如紅目鰱生魚片、比目魚生魚片，如果鮪魚是當季的，我也會點。還有放了鮮蝦、螺肉、九孔和血蛤的海鮮拼盤都很讚。

B At the restaurant we usually go to, our favorite dishes are baked shrimp, stir fried cabbage, steamed crab, stir fried lily flowers and seafood pumpkin soup.

在我們常去的海鮮餐廳，我們喜歡點焗烤蝦、炒高麗菜、清蒸花蟹、炒百合和南瓜海鮮湯。

C I am actually allergic to seafood. I stay away from all seafood. But I had a few non seafood dishes at a seafood restaurant that were really good. There is a sweet dessert called Ba Si (Wiredrawing). It is deep fried yam. It is coated with maltose. Before eating it, you deep it in cold water, the maltose will become crunchy.

我其實對海鮮過敏，所以我通常不會吃海鮮，但是我有在海鮮店吃過非海鮮的東西也很不錯。有一種甜點叫拔絲，就是地瓜炸過後裹上熱麥芽糖，吃的時候將地瓜過一下冰水，裹在外層的麥芽就會變得香脆可口。

1 北台灣的文化風情

2 中台灣的魅力風情

3 南台灣的熱力風情

4 東台灣農村風情

Q3 Is fresh tuna very expensive in Pingtung County?
新鮮鮪魚在屏東很貴嗎？

A Well no, I don't find it expensive, given the high quality of product.

哦，不會，我並不覺得貴，因為是高品質的肉。

B I do not mind paying a little more than I do for some other protein sources because it is a delicious treat and because if it was less expensive, the local fishermen might be tempted to break international fishing agreements in order to make a profit.

這會比其他一些蛋白質來源貴一點，但我不介意多付，因為很美味。如果是比較便宜的話，當地漁民可能會忍不住打破國際漁業協定，以賺取利潤。

C Normally, the restaurant chefs and street vendors purchase an entire fish. I don't know how much it would cost If a home cook wanted to buy a kilogram of fresh blue fin tuna to prepare. The price might depend on market demand and supply.

正常情況下，餐廳的廚師和街頭攤販都購買一整隻魚。我不知道如果一個家庭主婦想買新鮮黑鮪魚會是多少錢，這可能跟市場的供需會有關係。

 ## *Information* 美食報馬仔

位於屏東縣東港鎮光復路的「阿仁海產店」是東港黑鮪魚有名的海鮮餐廳，黑鮪魚生魚片、鐵辦黑鮪魚、油魷魚、櫻花蝦飛魚卵炒飯都是高人氣的菜。屏東縣東港鎮光復路「張家食堂」連續幾年標到第一尾鮪魚，張家食堂是不隨世俗流行貨真價值的東港美食。值得推薦的有：黑鮪魚生魚片、黑鮪魚菲力、櫻花蝦炒飯、櫻花蝦巧克力和南瓜海鮮湯。

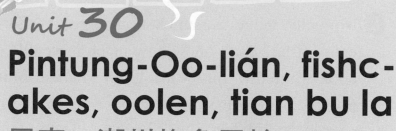

Unit 30
Pintung-Oo-lián, fishcakes, oolen, tian bu la
屏東－潮州旗魚黑輪

 ## Attractions 景點報報

石門古戰場位於車城鄉及牡丹鄉交界處，入口處停車場就可以走多達 396 階的長長的階梯。石門山有兩個登山口，從北登口進入的叫「石門山步道」，由南登口進入的叫「轉播台步道」。石門山可上可以看到觀音山、虎頭山、三台山等，甚至可以看到遠方的大海，因為有天然險障的地理關係，而成為軍事要地。「牡丹社事件」就發生在屏東牡丹的石門古戰場，也是排灣族牡丹社及高士佛社原住民對抗日軍入侵的地方。

 ## Popular snacks / street food 人氣小吃報報

Fish cake or oolen/tian bu la is a savory fried fish cake, primarily made of a paste of various types of seafood, potato starch, sugar, and pepper. The ingredients are ground and mashed into a smooth mixture, then shaped into a log for frying. The result is a springy, slightly chewy texture – that "Q" that is so important and popular in Taiwanese cuisine. Normally, the fried fish cake is served on a stick with a sweet and sour sauce. These fried fish cakes, along with fish balls and other delicacies are also available floating in a soup – inspired by the Japanese, as are fish cakes themselves. Pintung County, on the southernmost tip of Taiwan, is home to beautiful natural parks, seaports, and unique coral beaches. It is also the location where, in 1874, the Japanese landed and won bloody victories against the local tribes. This was the beginning of a twenty-year war for the island, won ultimately by the Japanese. This early battle is memorialized at the historic site ShiMen Ancient Battlefield. Though the site's memorials are somber, the mountainous landscape is breath-taking. Beautiful temples, artist colonies, tribal grounds and many other fascinating attractions are available throughout Pintung.

 中譯

　　黑輪是一種用魚漿做的美味油炸小吃，主要由各類海鮮、馬鈴薯澱粉、糖和胡椒粉所做。把混合均勻的麵糊做成長條狀後再油炸。這樣做出來的黑輪就是很有彈性、耐嚼感，也就是大家喜歡的台灣美食的「Q」感。黑輪的吃法是串在竹子上，加上甜酸醬。通常是煮一大鍋黑輪，搭配魚丸和其他食材，這種靈感來自於日本人的小吃。屏東縣位在台灣的最南端，這裡有美麗的自然公園、海港和獨特的珊瑚海灘。這裡也是 1874 年日本軍隊抵達後與當地部落作戰的地方。原住民在這個島嶼與日本人對抗二十多年的戰爭，最後由日本人戰勝。這個早期的戰鬥歷史的紀念遺址就是現在的石門古戰場。雖然紀念史蹟是嚴肅的，這裡的山區景觀卻是讓人驚歎。整個屏東地方都可以看到美麗的寺廟、藝術家集聚、部落地方和其他許多迷人丰采的景觀。

Q1 What kinds of fish are used in making these fish cakes?

黑輪是用什麼樣的魚做的呢？

🅐 Every vendor will have their own preference about that. Here near the ports, there are so many good, fresh choices.

每個店家都會有自己偏好的魚。這裡很靠近港口，所以有很多好又新鮮的魚可選擇。

🅑 Usually the vendor will select fish that are very fresh but also at a good price. Swordfish, mackerel, octopus and shrimp are all common ingredients.

通常情況下，店家會選擇非常新鮮，但價格也要好的魚。旗魚、鯖魚、魷魚和蝦都是常見的成分。

C Here in Taiwan, the standard fish for something like this is milk fish. If you decide to make them at home, you can use cod, haddock, or any white fish.

在台灣，一般常見的做法是用虱目魚。如果你要自己在家裡做，你可以用鱈魚、黑線鱈，或任何白肉魚。

1 北台灣的文化風情

2 中台灣的魅力風情

3 南台灣的熱力風情

4 東台灣農村風情

Q2 Are these similar to fish balls in any way?
黑輪跟一般魚丸很類似嗎？

A If you have had fresh fish balls in soup, then yes they are similar. The difference is that the fish paste is formed into a ball and then boiled in water or broth, whereas fish cakes are shaped into logs and fried. The same fish paste can be used.

如果你吃過魚丸湯，其實是相似的。不同的是，魚丸是做成圓球狀後在水中煮，而黑輪則是做成長條狀再去油炸。魚漿的麵糊其實一樣。

B The fish paste can be really the same for either dish, but I so prefer the crunchy outside and the springy inside of the fish cake!

這兩種魚漿的麵糊是相同的，但我比較喜歡外皮吃起來脆脆，裡面有彈性的的黑輪！

C Fish balls are always floating in soup when eaten, right? These fried fish cakes can float in soup too, but the easier way to eat them while window-shopping in the street market is on a stick. Plus the sweet and sour dipping sauce really makes them delicious!

魚丸通常是煮湯吃，對嗎？黑輪也可以用來煮湯，但是串在竹籤上，逛街時吃會比較方便。再加上甜辣醬才真正好吃！

Q3 Is there any breading inside or outside of the fish cake? I can't eat any gluten.

魚漿的麵糊裡外是否有加任何麵包粉？我不能吃麵筋。

A I will ask the vendor for you. I don't think so, but I want to be sure so you don't get sick. My son is gluten intolerant and cannot have any wheat or corn products.

我會問問看。我覺得應該沒有，我不希望你吃了會生病，所以要確認一下。我的兒子也是麩質不耐症，不能吃有任何小麥或玉米的產品。

B No, these are made the traditional way with potato and rice flour. The pre-packaged ones from China might include cornstarch, but these are safe.

沒有，傳統方式是加馬鈴薯粉和米做的粉。從中國做的那種可能有加玉米澱粉，但這些都是安全的。

C There is no breading on the outside, but the vendor does add some starch to the inside to help the ground fish stick together. Normally, the starch is rice flour, though. Is that okay for you to eat?

外面沒有裹麵包粉,但店家會加一些澱粉添加到麵糊裡,這樣可以幫助魚肉和在一起。通常會加米做的粉。這樣你可以吃嗎?

Information 美食報馬仔

屏東縣潮州鎮除了大廟口旗魚黑輪外,瑞字號旗魚黑輪位在屏東縣東港鎮朝隆路(東港華僑市場內)也是赫赫有名。通常賣的東西一樣是有分水煮的關東煮和油炸的旗魚黑輪和甜不辣,也都會提供免費味噌湯,旗魚黑輪有包蛋跟沒有包蛋兩種,各有風味,也會賣多種的關東煮。值得一提的是,多種語言演變是很有意思的,從日文的發音到「黑輪」就變成台語加英文的「ΛΟ 戀」。

Part 4

東台灣
農村風情

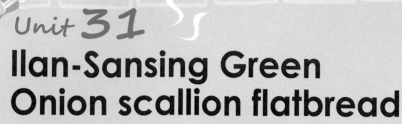

Unit 31
Ilan-Sansing Green Onion scallion flatbread
宜蘭－三星蔥油餅

 ## *Attractions* 景點報報

日治時代日本人在台灣的阿里山、八仙山與太平山興建森林鐵路主要是開採珍貴木材。宜蘭太平山有幾條特色步道，平原自然步道兩旁都是高大檜木，茂興步道可以看到許多神木，翠峰湖環湖步道可享受翠峰湖之美景，台灣山毛櫸國家步道可見到珍貴稀有的植物山毛櫸，見晴懷古步道可以觀望蘭陽平原和蘭陽溪，這條步道以前是運材鐵道，步道全長 2.35 公里，雪山山脈、桃山、大霸尖山都遠在天邊近在眼前。

 ## *Popular snacks / street food* 人氣小吃報報

One well-known and well-loved finger food in Taiwan is scallion flatbread. It uses such simple ingredients and preparation, though the result is so tasty! The cook prepares a basic wheat flour and water dough, rolls a large piece out to add oil, diced scallions and salt, then rolls small pieces into circles for pan-frying into flaky finger food. In Ilan and other areas of Taiwan, street vendors offer either plain or in a classic Taiwanese style with an egg. This treat arrived in Taiwan from mainland China when the imperial army and its supporters fled during the communist takeover. The origin of scallion flatbread – or sometimes called fried green onion pancake – is not specifically known. Some sources suppose that the Indian population of Beijing may have had a hand in developing this Chinese treat, since it is similar to a flatbread they loved from their cuisine, called paratha. Ilan county in the northeast coastal area of Taiwan was home to two aboriginal groups: a mountain settlement of Atayal people and a coastal and riverbank group of settlements by the Kavalan, after which the county is named. The best scallion flatbread is from Ilan where it grows the best green onion called Sansing Green Onion.

 中譯

　　蔥油餅是眾所皆知且深受大家喜愛的台灣小吃。雖然只是簡單的材料和做法，但就是非常好吃！做法是用基本的小麥粉和水做成麵團再桿成一大塊，在麵皮上加油、香蔥和鹽，捲成圓形狀，要煎之前再桿開好下鍋油煎，這就是有層次的蔥油餅。在宜蘭及台灣等地區，街頭攤販會賣一般或加蛋的蔥油餅。這種小吃是當時國民黨在大陸撤退逃離到台灣時所帶進來的小吃。蔥油餅或蔥花大餅並沒有考據的來源。有些來源指出在北京的印度人口對這個在中國的小吃有啟發的影響，因為這與印度人自己的印度大餅很類似。在台灣東北部沿海地區的宜蘭縣是兩個當地原住民：一是靠山的泰雅族人和沿海河岸而居的噶瑪蘭人，這也是宜蘭縣被命名的起源。最好的蔥油餅在宜蘭，因為這裡所生長的三星蔥是最棒的蔥。

Q1 **What time of day is the scallion flatbread normally consumed?**
通常蔥油餅都是什麼時候會吃呢？

A This is a very versatile dish – it could be a delicious hot breakfast, a snack between meals, or an appetizer before a larger meal.

這其實是很有變化性的小吃。可以當早餐、點心或者餐前的開胃菜。

B You can see vendors selling it in the morning, in the afternoon and at night market! Scallion flatbread vendors usually like to sell their food near schools. It is a cheap snack so students can easily afford it.

在上午、下午和夜市，不同時間都有人在賣蔥油餅！蔥油餅攤販通常喜歡在學校附近擺攤，因為這種便宜的小吃，學生都可以買得起。

C This flaky savory flatbread is something I loved to eat on the way to high school. The dough is fried and crispy. The smell and taste of scallion is just so satisfying when you are hungry to eat it.

這種有多層餅皮的蔥油餅是我上高中時最喜歡吃的小吃。外皮煎得金黃酥脆，咬下一口，吃到的蔥的香氣和味道馬上令人覺得很滿足。

1 北台灣的文化風情

2 中台灣的魅力風情

3 南台灣的熱力風情

4 東台灣農村風情

Q2　How does the flatbread become so flaky?
為何蔥油餅皮會一層一層的呢？

A Some scallion flatbread is not flaky. It is just rolled-out dough, fried with egg and green onions. It is not flaky but it is just as good.

有些蔥油餅沒有層次，就只是擀開餅皮，和蛋、蔥一起油炸，皮是沒有一層層的，但有蔥味就好吃。

B I have heard that using a good quality wheat flour, plus allowing the dough to rest before rolling it out really makes it nice and light.

我聽說使用好的麵粉是重點，尤其擀開麵團前先醒麵，麵皮才會好吃也鬆軟。

C Do you know how French croissants are made? This is very similar – dough rolled out, then coated with a fat layer that is then folded or rolled up to make alternating layers of fat and dough. This process is called "lamination," making the bread so crispy and light.

你知道法國羊角麵包嗎？做法與蔥油餅非常相似，都是把麵團開，然後塗上一層油脂後將其折疊或捲起，讓油脂和麵皮有交替的層次。這一過程被稱為「分層法」，可以讓麵包香脆又鬆軟。

1 北台灣的文化風情

2 中台灣的魅力風情

3 南台灣的熱力風情

4 東台灣農村風情

Tell me more about the dipping sauce used for this bread.

請可以告訴我蔥油餅的沾醬是怎麼做的。

A There can be some variety, but all have soy sauce and sesame oil. Scallion flatbread in Ilan is different than the south. The delicious Sansing Green Onions really are phenomenal. You only need to brush lightly with soy sauce on the crispy flatbread.

有很多不同類型的沾醬,但裡面都有加醬油和香油。宜蘭的蔥油餅跟中南部的口味有點不一樣,可口的三星蔥真的很驚人,簡單刷上醬油就很好吃!

B Different vendors have their own recipes, though I really prefer it when the sauce has a tomato base, made spicy with red pepper sauce and also made sweet with sugar.

不同的攤販有自己的做法,但我比較喜歡加番茄醬、紅辣椒醬和糖那種辣辣甜甜的沾醬。

C Well, this one looks like it has soy sauce, sesame oil, and some ginger or garlic. I do like this kind. It is the perfect accent for the warm, flaky scallion flatbread.

這個看起來像是有加醬油、香油和一些生薑或大蒜。我喜歡這個味道。這和熱熱外層酥脆蔥油餅很配。

 ## Information 美食報馬仔

　　宜蘭員山的阿肥蔥油餅有獨具特色的蔥油餅，使用員山韭菜的韭菜盒也是賣點。頭城車站阿公蔥油餅賣蔥油餅捐贈消防警備車是大街小巷熟悉的溫馨故事。三星阿婆蔥油餅是得過宜蘭冠軍蔥油餅的知名老店，阿婆的冠軍小珊餅鹹鹹甜甜的，因為加了培根、麻糬和三星蔥。就在斜對面的何家蔥餡餅是高人氣的老店。宜蘭礁溪老字號的柯氏蔥油餅是排隊美食，宜蘭東門夜市必吃的美食是彭記蔥油餅。

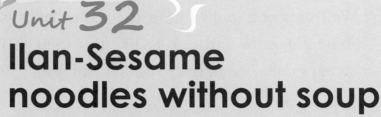

Unit 32
Ilan-Sesame noodles without soup
宜蘭－麻醬乾麵

🏛️ *Attractions* 景點報報

　　宜蘭的馬告國家公園可以看到不少珍貴的神木群，這裡的神木大多是紅檜和扁柏，屬於台灣原生珍貴的樹種。電影賽德克巴萊有部分在此取景。在日據時代和國民政府的砍伐前，這裡的生態處處都是原生種的木材。馬告在泰雅族話是野生山胡椒，這個材料可以增加特殊氣味。馬告的味道類似薑、檸檬和黑胡椒的混合味道。馬告國家公園跟龜山島一樣是管制區。

Popular snacks / street food 人氣小吃報報

Sesame noodles are a popular breakfast choice in Ilan. Sesame noodles are just a bowl of noodles without soup that is mixed with sesame paste, peanut butter, sugar, salt and water. Another type of popular noodles is simple as it can be. It is cooked noodles mixed with fried shallots, soy sauce and black vinegar. Although sesame noodles look vegan, it might not be. If you are a vegan and do not eat meat, eggs, or dairy of any kind, you want to double check with the vendor. Lard is a common ingredient in many foods. The noodles may be egg noodles, depending on what the cook prefers. When the ingredient is fried shallots, it is mostly fried with lard. Ilan is situated in the northeast quadrant of the island of Taiwan – less than an hour's drive from Taipei. Visitors and residents enjoy lush tropical mountain scenery, including waterfalls and hiking trails, beautiful sandy ocean beaches and sparsely populated agricultural areas. Numerous hot and cold springs provide public bathing opportunities, though only the most brave and hardy would venture into a 50 degree Celsius (122 Fahrenheit) whole-body bath!

 中譯

　　麻醬乾麵在宜蘭是很流行的早餐。麻醬乾麵是芝麻醬、花生醬、糖、鹽和開水攪拌均勻，拌入煮熟的麵條即可。另外一種沒有特別醬料的麵只是白麵加上油蔥頭、醬油和黑醋就是一碗簡單特別好吃的麵。儘管麻醬乾麵看起來像全素，但很可能不是全素。如果你是素食主義者，你不吃肉、蛋或任何形式的乳製品，要吃前還是先跟賣家確認一下材料。豬油是許多烹煮的常見成分。麵條可能是雞蛋做的麵，就看店家喜歡用什麼樣的麵。如果成分説是油蔥頭，其實大多是用豬油炸過的。宜蘭位於台灣島的東北，從台北開車不到一小時的車程。遊客和當地居民喜歡宜蘭好山好水的熱帶風光，包括瀑布和步行健道、美麗海洋沙灘，以及疏稀的農業地。這裡有許多冷熱溫泉可以提供公共溫泉，但應該只有少數勇敢和健壯的人會泡到攝氏 50 度（華氏 122 度）的溫泉吧！

Q & A 外國人都是這樣問))) *MP3 32*

Q1 **Do they just offer sesame noodles? Anything else?**
店家只有賣麻醬乾麵嗎？還有其他的嗎？

A Yes. There are other noodles without soup. These are just noodles mixed with lard and salt or noodles with satay. This looks very easy to make but only experienced vendors know how to make the simple ingredients to their utmost taste.

有的，還有賣其他乾麵類。這些純粹是乾麵拌豬油和鹽，或是半沙茶。越是簡單的搭配組合，才真的能看出店家的功力！

B They also have noodles with soup. Do you want to try wonton noodles and preserved greens and sliced meat noodles?

他們還有賣湯麵類。你想試試餛飩麵和榨菜肉絲麵嗎？

C People in Taiwan like to have a bowl of soup with their order of noodles. Vendors usually offer different types of soup such as clam soup, pig intestine soup, wonton soup, meatball soup or even pig brain soup.

台灣人喜歡吃乾麵外加喝湯，通常賣乾麵的店也會賣蛤蜊湯、豬腸湯、餛飩湯、貢丸湯，魚丸湯甚至豬腦髓湯。

The noodles are a little chewier than I'm used to. Why is that?

這個麵吃起來比我習慣吃的較有咬勁，為什麼呢？

A Taiwanese people love chewy noodles! You can even read the packages of dry noodles in the store to find out how chewy they are. The code for chewy is "Q" and extra chewy is "QQ!" I think these are QQ.

台灣人喜歡吃有嚼勁的麵！甚至在包裝乾麵上會寫説麵條的嚼勁度。對於有嚼勁的代碼是「Q」，更是有嚼勁的代碼是「QQ！」。我覺得這碗麵是 QQ 的程度。

B If the noodles weren't chewy, the dish of just sauce and noodles would be like eating mushy – and spicy – oatmeal. Very strange to me.

如果麵條沒有嚼勁，這道菜就只是醬料和麵條，會像吃糊狀和辣辣的燕麥片一樣。我覺得很奇怪。

C We enjoy a chewy, springy texture to our food. Have you had bubble tea? Those tapioca balls are not there for flavor, but for texture. Taiwanese really like this experience of having to work at chewing certain things. Maybe the appeal is a little like your gummy bear candy in the west?

我們喜歡吃有嚼勁，彈性的口感。你有喝過波霸奶茶嗎？那一粒粒用木薯粉做的粉圓其實沒有什麼味道，但口感很棒。台灣人真的很喜歡吃的時候有咀嚼的口感。也許就像在美國你喜歡吃的橡皮糖小熊軟糖一樣。

1 北台灣的文化風情

2 中台灣的魅力風情

3 南台灣的熱力風情

4 東台灣農村風情

Q3 Does this dish have sesame oil in the sauce?

麻醬乾麵是否有加香油？

A No, normally it is roasted sesame paste, mixed together with natural peanut butter.

沒有，通常是由烤過的芝麻所做的芝麻醬，和天然的花生醬混合在一起。

B It's such a good flavor, isn't it? Some cooks may use sesame oil because it is so easily available and is used for many other dishes in Taiwan.

味道很棒對不對？有些是會加香油，因為這個材料很容易取得，在台灣很多菜裡都有加香油。

C The sesame oil with the vinegar and other flavors make the sauce just wonderfully refreshing.

香油加醋和其他材料真的就讓味道很清爽。

Information 美食報馬仔

　　宜蘭必吃的銅板美食是麻醬麵、炸醬麵和乾拌麵。位在羅東南路門上的無名麵店完全沒有招牌，也非常不顯眼，這是在地老饕推薦的超美味的乾麵，網友直接把這家麵店稱為「羅東無名好吃乾麵」。宜蘭冬山鄉廣興村廣興路的羅東帝爺廟口嗹咕麵、宜蘭市中心文昌路的文昌炸醬麵、頭城的綵宸小吃店，還有陽明醫院對面的正宗老牌大麵章的麻醬麵都是在地人的推薦美食。

Unit 33
Ilan-fish ball and rice noodle soup
宜蘭－魚丸米粉

 Attractions 景點報報

　　宜蘭跑馬古道是在烏來鄉與宜蘭縣的界線，全長約 6.5 公里，古道上山明水秀，途中可眺望龜山島及蘭陽平原。這是一個坡度和緩，又很受歡迎的登山健行步道，也有不少植物解說牌。走完跑馬古道後可以去位於礁溪鄉林美地區的林美石磐步道，全長約 1700 公尺，沿途步道會看到石壁與瀑布，稱為石盤瀑布，這是屬於環形步道，沿途林蔭遮天和瀑布流水是避暑好去處。

 Popular snacks / street food 人氣小吃報報

Tofu (or Dou Fu) and other soy products like fresh or frozen green soybeans for eating, soy sauce and soy milk are important staples in Taiwanese kitchens and are plentiful in street vendors' stalls. Taiwan is within the top 10 countries in soybean consumption in the world. Almost 10 percent of Taiwan's arable land is planted to soybeans, yet 97 percent of the soy Taiwan needs is imported from other countries. In fact, US soybeans account for 55 percent of what Taiwan imports of this high protein snack, condiment or main dish. Small scale manufacturers still make bean curd by hand and deliver it to markets and restaurants every morning. The process for making bean curd involves soaking soy beans, grinding them, straining off the soy milk, then coagulating what is left before placing the semi-solid remainder into a mold so that it can "set." Once tofu is made, it is eatable. It can also be made into different products. Oily tofu is fried tofu, which is popularly added in soups or hot pot in Taiwan. Fried tofu is a key ingredient in making an authentic bowl of fish and noodle soup in Ilan.

 中譯

　　豆腐或其他豆製品如用來吃的新鮮或冷凍毛豆、醬油和豆漿都是在台灣的家庭或路邊攤烹煮的重要食材。台灣是全世界消費黃豆排名前 10 名的國家。台灣的耕地有近 10％是種植黃豆，而台灣所需要的黃豆有 97％是從其他國家進口的。事實上，美國的黃豆佔台灣進口量的 55％，黃豆是高蛋白的來源，也可做調味品或主菜。小規模的豆腐生產廠家還是有人用手工做豆腐，每天早晨提供給市場和餐館。豆腐的製作方法包括浸泡大豆，研磨，過濾豆漿，凝固後把半成品放入模型「成型」。一旦豆腐做好了，可以馬上食用，也可以做成不同產品。油豆腐可以放入湯或火鍋，在台灣這都是流行的吃法。油豆腐是宜蘭魚丸米粉的一個關鍵食材。

Q & A 外國人都是這樣問 🔊 *MP3 33*

Q1 **Tofu has such a weird texture. I don't think I'll like fried tofu.**

豆腐吃起來很奇怪，我不覺得我會喜歡這個油豆腐。

A I hear many westerners say that, but perhaps it is because you have never had it prepared properly? If you are going to like tofu anywhere, it will be here in Taiwan. Would you try it and see what you think?

我是聽過很多西方人這樣說過，但也許那是因為你從未吃過正確煮法的油豆腐？如果你要去會喜歡吃豆腐的地方，就是在台灣。你要不要試一下後再說說你的想法？

B The texture may be a little "Q" or chewy and surprising for you. I think that just gives your mouth more time to enjoy the flavor of the sauce around the tofu!

口感可能會有點「Q」或有咬勁，你吃起來會覺得很驚訝。我認為這只是讓你的嘴裡有更多的時間來可以享受豆腐的味道！

C Fried tofu and meatballs go well together in soup. The fried tofu has a good smell and it absorbs the soup. It is really good. Would you like to try some of this soup to see if you like it? The fish ball is also very Q. Chopped celery and fried shallots are added on the top before serving.

油豆腐跟魚丸很配。油豆腐本身香氣十足，內裡又吸飽湯汁，真的很好吃。你要不要先試試看再說？魚丸也是相當 Q 彈，上桌前再加上芹菜和油蔥，真的很香。

1 北台灣的文化風情

2 中台灣的魅力風情

3 南台灣的熱力風情

4 東台灣農村風情

Q2 Where are the soybeans grown that are eventually turned into tofu here in Taiwan?

在台灣用來做豆腐的黃豆都是在哪裡種植的呢？

A Some are grown on the island, but there is not much agricultural land here due to the mountains and the large industrial cities. So, Taiwan imports almost all of its soybeans from other countries.

有一些是在台灣島上種植，但因為山脈和工業城市發展的關係，所以現在台灣已經沒有太多的農業用地。因此，幾乎所有台灣的黃豆都是從其他國家進口的。

B Why do you ask? Is your family connected to farming soybeans in your home country? Maybe we are going to eat some that came from your family farm.

你為什麼問呢？在你的家鄉跟種植黃豆有關嗎？也許我們會吃到一些是從你的家庭農場來的黃豆。

C The dry soybeans normally come from the U.S., Australia, or mainland Asia. The Taiwanese people are glad to be able to find enough soybeans to satisfy the large amount of soy that we eat!

乾的黃豆一般是從美國、澳大利亞或亞洲大陸進口的。台灣人很高興能夠找到足夠的黃豆，來滿足我們對黃豆的大量需求！

Q3 Are the thick rice noodles in the fish and noodle soup only found in Ilan?
宜蘭魚丸米粉裡的粗米粉只有在宜蘭才有嗎？

A I have seen it in other places in northern Taiwan but hardly seen it in the south. Vendors in Ilan mostly use this type of thick noodles. It became a specialty in Ilan. After it is cooked, the thick noodles sort of break it up. It can cook over high heat without being too mushy.

其他北部地方應該有，南部比較少見。宜蘭賣魚丸米粉的幾乎都是用粗米粉，這也成了宜蘭的特產，經過烹煮後，粗米粉會斷裂也是特色之一。粗米粉可以高溫久煮不糊爛。

B I honestly don't know. This is the first time I have tried this type of thick rice noodles.

我其實真的不知道。我是第一次吃到這種粗米粉。

C Unlike dry noodles, it can directly be added to soup base without pre-cooking in hot water.

可以直接加入高湯，不像乾的米粉要先在熱水中煮。

 ### *Information* 美食報馬仔

　　魚丸米粉是宜蘭人早餐的其中一個選項。在民權新路口，開漳聖王廟旁阿添魚丸米粉是在地的高人氣早餐，也有單賣魚丸外帶。老福魚丸米粉就在宜蘭市區東門夜市旁邊，店裡有提供推薦的吃法就是「麻辣魯肉飯」、「魚丸米粉招牌辣」。其他如楊彩卿魚丸米粉、信利號貓耳魚丸米粉都是有名的在地老店。正宗的魚丸米粉裡用的米粉是粗短的米粉，有別於一般米粉。

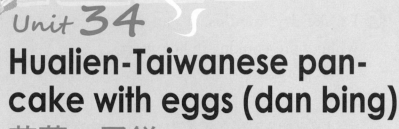

Unit 34
Hualien-Taiwanese pancake with eggs (dan bing)
花蓮－蛋餅

 Attractions 景點報報

花蓮七星潭自行車道全長十五公里，起點是南濱公園，沿途會經過太平洋公園、曙光橋，花蓮縣和平廣場，江口良三郎紀念公園還有台肥海洋深層水園區，水園區裡有觀星亭與聽海亭。也會經過有一片大草原的「軍事要塞」但這裡是重要軍事管制區。〔七星潭〕是一個海灣，海岸風光優美，讓人陶醉不已。沿著七星潭的月牙灣，最後會到達自行車道的起點。

 Popular snacks / street food 人氣小吃報報

Anyone who has visited Taiwan has probably tried Taiwanese pancake with egg for breakfast. And if they've tried it once they've either sought it out again or mastered making this simple dish at home. Even in a mountainous place like Hualien, dan bing is a popular choice for breakfast. The pancake starts as unleavened flatbread dough, cooked quickly in a skillet or large round flat pan. It is sometimes also made with a thinner crepe-like batter. A couple of well-beaten eggs are also cooked into a flat circle and once you roll the two things together, that's dan bing! Diced green onions are also either in the pancake or the egg and a delicious brown sauce of soy and sugar really makes the dan bing sing. Customers might have the option to add bacon or ham, cooked seafood corn, pork floss. Many visitors to Hualien come for visiting the famous Taroko National Park. The park, one of nine national parks in the country, is perhaps Taiwan's most popular natural area, and was named after the magnificent marble-faced gorge, Taroko Gorge. The gorge is named for the Taroko or Truku Tribe, one of the 16 officially recognized aboriginal groups of the island.

 中譯

　　任何去過台灣的人可能已經吃過早餐有加雞蛋的蛋餅。有吃過的人，可能會想再吃一次，或試著自己在家做這道簡單的菜。即使是像花蓮這樣多山的地方，蛋餅也是很多人的早餐選擇。蛋餅是用無發酵的麵團所做的，在煎鍋或平底鍋快速煎熟。蛋餅皮也可以用麵糊來做。打個雞蛋加在餅皮上，這就是蛋餅！有些做法是蔥末加在餅皮裡，有些做法是加在蛋裡。蛋餅做好後再淋上醬汁，就是好吃的蛋餅。顧客有時可以選擇添加培根或火腿、海鮮玉米或肉鬆。許多遊客會到花蓮拜訪著名的太魯閣國家公園。太魯閣是台灣的 9 個國家公園之一，或許也是台灣最受歡迎的自然景觀，太魯閣峽谷這名字因為其宏偉的大理石峽谷，而也因為原住民太魯閣定居在這裡，才叫做太魯閣國家公園。

Q1 What is this sweet brown sauce made of?
這種甜甜棕色的醬是什麼做的？

🅐 Normally, it is soy sauce, ketchup, sugar, garlic, water and starch to thicken. Isn't it yummy?

一般來說是醬油、番茄醬、糖、蒜加水煮滾後用加澱粉調稠。是不是很美味？

🅑 I've seen different people make it a little differently – some use oyster sauce, some use a little Coca-Cola, some even make it spicy – all have soy sauce, sugar, and ketchup though.

我見過不同的做法- 有的用蠔油，有的用一點可口可樂，有的甚至是辣味的，但這些都是有加醬油，糖和番茄醬。

C It is a little bit one of those recipes that is a well-kept secret. No vendor wants to tell you how they make their own special sauce! I can taste soy and garlic though and it is definitely sweet not savory. Can you taste any other ingredients?

通常醬汁是賣家的祕方。賣家不會願意說出他們如何做自己特製的醬汁的！我是可以吃到醬油和大蒜的味道，這絕對是屬於甜醬，而非鹹醬。你還有吃到什麼材料嗎？

1 北台灣的文化風情

2 中台灣的魅力風情

3 南台灣的熱力風情

4 東台灣農村風情

Q2 How is this different from French crepes?
這跟法式薄餅有什麼不同？

A I'm not familiar at all with French crepes. Could you describe them for me and I will see how they are different and how they are similar to dan bing.

我不知道什麼是法式薄餅。你可以描述給我聽聽，這樣我可能就知道和蛋餅的異同處。

B If I understand what French crepes are, I can say that these Taiwanese pancakes with egg are different because they are savory with a sweet sauce where French crepes are often all sweet or all savory – almost never a combination.

如果沒錯的話，我所知道的法式薄餅與蛋餅應該不一樣。台灣的蛋餅是有加蛋還有甜甜酸酸好吃的醬，法式薄餅薄餅往往都是甜的或鹹的，不太可能會把這兩種味道組合在一起。

C Crepes are always made from a thin batter, isn't that right? Taiwanese pancakes are often made from a flatbread dough or a batter.

可麗餅也是稀麵糊做的，不是嗎？台灣蛋餅通常是用餅麵團或用麵糊做的。

Q3 What kinds of fillings do you recommend for dan bing?
你推薦蛋餅加什麼樣的料？

A If you want to be safe and traditional, then order just the egg. It's really very delicious and comforting in its simplicity.

如果你要確定好吃又傳統的話，就加蛋。這真的是很簡單，非常好吃也很有飽足感。

B Well, that is your choice. What types of things do you like to eat: Bacon? Corn? You can even add processed cheese to the dish, though clearly the cheese version is a nod to western tastes.

嗯，這是你的選擇。你喜歡什麼口味，培根？玉米？也可以加起司，雖然很明顯的起司是西方口味。

C I really like those that add corn and bacon to the egg. Oh, and a little cilantro. So hearty and fresh tasting at the same time. I don't get hungry for hours!

我真的很喜歡加蛋後再加玉米和培根。哦，還有加一點香菜。吃起來就是痛快又清爽，肚子可以感到飽足好幾個小時！

 ## *Information* 美食報馬仔

　　位在花蓮市南京街的巷子裡 的怡味餐店是當地人氣很夯的早餐店。雖然賣的東西與是一般早餐店差不多，但每一項都做得實實在在讓人豎起大拇指。煎餃、煎包、傳統蛋餅都是現點現煎。煎餃的餡料是用韭菜或高麗菜加上鮮肉口感很紮實，類似煎餃的燒賣不是用蒸的而是用煎的。必點的是傳統蛋餅，蛋餅餅皮是用麵粉現桿現煎，味噌湯與鮮奶茶也是人人稱讚，而且價格都相當經濟實惠。

文法/生活英語 003

跟著小吃用英語晒台灣（附 MP3）

作　　　者	林昭菁	
發 行 人	周瑞德	
執行總監	齊心瑀	
行銷經理	楊景輝	
企劃編輯	陳欣慧	
執行編輯	陳韋佑	
封面構成	高鍾琪	

內頁構成	菩薩蠻數位文化有限公司
印　　製	大亞彩色印刷製版股份有限公司
初　　版	2017 年 6 月
定　　價	新台幣 380 元
出　　版	倍斯特出版事業有限公司
電　　話	(02) 2351-2007
傳　　真	(02) 2351-0887
地　　址	100 台北市中正區福州街 1 號 10 樓之 2
E - m a i l	best.books.service@gmail.com
網　　址	www.bestbookstw.com

港澳地區總經銷	泛華發行代理有限公司
地　　　址	香港新界將軍澳工業邨駿昌街 7 號 2 樓
電　　話	(852) 2798-2323
傳　　真	(852) 2796-5471

國家圖書館出版品預行編目(CIP)資料

跟著小吃用英語晒台灣 / 林昭菁著. -- 初
版. -- 臺北市 : 倍斯特, 2017.06 面 ;
公分. --（文法/生活英語 ; 3）
ISBN 978-986-94428-5-5(平裝附光碟片)1.
英語 2.會話 3.讀本

805.188　　　　　　　　106006593